DEAD RINGER

When Lizzie Holden drives a wagon into the town of Jacob's Creek, Connor Riordan is smitten. Though she is betrothed to Jeremiah Newham, Lizzie slowly begins to realise her fiancé is not all he seems. And her arrival has inspired disquiet amongst the townsfolk. For Lizzie bears a striking resemblance to Elizabeth King, a young woman who turned down a rich suitor to marry one of her father's ranch hands — and perished when her homestead was burned to the ground . . .

SARAH SWATRIDGE

DEAD RINGER

Complete and Unabridged

LINFORD
Leicester

First published in Great Britain in 2019

First Linford Edition
published 2020

A catalogue record for this book is available
from the British Library.

ISBN 978–1–4448–4584–6

Published by
Ulverscroft Limited
Anstey, Leicestershire

Set by Words & Graphics Ltd.
Anstey, Leicestershire
Printed and bound in Great Britain by
TJ Books Limited, Padstow, Cornwall

This book is printed on acid-free paper

Just Passing Through

Connor stared at the wagon as it grew closer. He'd noticed the torn fabric from the bullet holes, but that wasn't any reason to stop and stare. It was Lizzie Holden sitting up high and steering it into town as if she'd been born to do the job. Her hair was blown back by the breeze and she had a carefree air about her.

May, Connor's sister, was standing beside him.

'She's pretty,' she teased. 'Not seen the likes of her round here before.'

'I ain't so sure about that,' Connor said.

'She does look a bit like Elizabeth from up at High Point, now you come to mention it.'

'A real dead ringer for Elizabeth King if you ask me.'

Lizzie pulled on the reins and steered

1

the horses to the side of the dirt track and brought them to a halt outside the town's only hotel and saloon bar.

Nimbly she slipped down and tied them up, affectionately giving one of the horses a friendly pat on the side. She walked round the wagon and helped out firstly a mature woman who was followed closely by a young man.

Connor couldn't tear his eyes away from the tiny frame of the young woman. He liked what he saw. What a beauty! Dainty she might be, but watching her she seemed as strong as an ox and capable with it.

The young man reached for their cases but had a fit of coughing, and it was Lizzie who carried them in. All three of them made their way into the town's hotel and waited at the desk.

'Is she their servant?' Connor muttered to himself. May gave him a surprised look.

'She is their equal. No doubt about it.'

'And what makes you so sure?' he asked.

May gave it some thought before answering her brother.

'I think it's the way she carries herself. She looks confident to me,' May said rather wistfully, 'like Miss Harper at school.'

Connor chuckled as he recalled his school days and his initial fear of Miss Harper which grew into respect.

★ ★ ★

'I think you ought to stand closer to Lizzie,' Susanna Newham, the older of the two women, whispered to the young man. 'All the men seem to be looking at her as if they haven't seen a young woman in years. You'd better be careful or she'll have them all setting their caps at her.'

'She's a beautiful girl,' Jeremiah, the young man, said absently as though he took her beauty for granted. 'I suppose I'll have to get used to jealous men.'

He stood proudly beside an oblivious Lizzie. She was more interested in looking around the entrance to the hotel than the effect she was having on the town's male folk.

'We need two rooms,' the older woman was saying. 'One for myself, Mrs Susanna Newham and Miss Holden here, and one for my son, Jeremiah Newham.'

'And how long might you be staying?' Daniel Bradley, the bearded old man behind the counter, asked.

'We're just here for the night. We're on our way up the creek early in the morning,' she explained.

The young man let out a loud sneeze as he and Lizzie gathered together their cases and followed his mother to their rooms. The ladies freshened up and combed each other's hair.

'Aren't you going to unpack anything?' Susanna asked Lizzie who was busy looking out of the window.

'I wasn't going to,' she answered. 'We're only here for the night. It doesn't seem worth the trouble.'

'What are you looking at?' Susanna asked as she approached the window which looked down into the town square.

'Just looking,' Lizzie said. 'I've never been here before so I guess I'm curious. That's all.'

Susanna peered out. A horse was drinking from the trough but other than that the place was deserted.

'I'd love to go and have a walk round,' Lizzie said, looking appealingly at Susanna.

'Well, go and knock on Jeremiah's door and see if he'll oblige,' she suggested. 'You'll need an escort in a town like this.'

Lizzie didn't need to be told twice. She spun round and out of the door, along the narrow corridor to Jeremiah's room. She knocked enthusiastically but there was no reply. She tried once more before returning to her own room and to her companion.

'He's gone,' she told Susanna. 'At

5

least, there was no reply.'

'That's odd,' Susanna said, looking up from folding her dress. 'Perhaps he's gone into town for a shave, although I'd have thought he'd let us know he was going out. I will just go and check on him. He's been very quiet today and not really himself. I think he's a bit out of sorts.'

Susanna made her way to his room. She knocked on his door and, being his mother, turned the handle and marched in just to be sure it was empty.

Jeremiah groaned as the light from the corridor filtered into his room. He was curled up in bed feeling very sorry for himself.

'I'm burning up,' he moaned. 'I feel so awful. Just leave me be.'

'Let me see,' Susanna said as she touched his forehead. He was clammy and hot, yet his skin looked pale. 'Best thing you can do is to sleep it off,' she told him. 'Lizzie and I are going out to get a bit of fresh air and have something to eat. Do you want anything?'

'Just let me sleep.' He groaned and rolled over, pulling the covers over him.

Susanna returned to her room only to find Lizzie at the window again watching the world go by.

'Jeremiah's in his room,' she told the young girl. 'He's not well. He's got a bit of a fever and he's going to sleep it off, but we can go and get a bit of fresh air and stretch our legs after that long journey. I can see you're champing at the bit to go and explore.'

'Will it be all right to leave him?' Lizzie asked in concern. 'I mean, does he need me to nurse him?'

Susanna laughed.

'He'll be fine. He's been coughing and sneezing all day. A good sleep will see him right.'

'If you say so,' Lizzie said. 'I just don't like to think of him being ill and me not being there when he needs me.'

'A commendable statement, young lady, but don't start fussing over him or he'll enjoy being ill and you won't want a sickly husband, believe me.'

Lizzie turned and was about to ask about the late Mr Newham, of whom she knew very little, but there was something about the brisk manner in which Susanna was getting ready to go out that made her hold her tongue.

One day, she was sure, she would learn about Jeremiah's father, but it seemed it was not going to be today.

It was late afternoon but, being early summer, there were still a few hours until the sun went down and the weather was pleasant enough for the two ladies to walk along the boardwalk from the hotel to the general store on the other side of the main street.

'My, they do stare around here,' Susanna said after a little while. 'Hasn't anyone ever seen a pretty lass here before?'

Lizzie pointed out the names above the door on a wooden plaque. It said, *General Store. Samuel and Mary Franklin welcome you in.*

But once inside, the woman who ran the store with her husband looked up, first at Susanna and then at Lizzie, and they, too, began to stare. That didn't seem much of a welcome to the two visitors.

'She's the image of our Elizabeth, God rest her soul,' the woman said, and they presumed she must be Mrs Mary Franklin. 'No wonder everyone's looking. It's like she's back from the dead.'

'I'm afraid you'll have to tell me more. We're strangers to the area and know nothing of its history,' Susanna told them. 'Who was this Elizabeth and what happened to her?'

'It's a tragic tale,' the woman said as she got comfortable on her wooden stool behind the counter. 'Now, let me think.' She stroked her chin.

'It would have been about twenty-five or so years ago, maybe a bit more. That's really when it all started. There was this pretty girl, Elizabeth, only daughter of Ma and Isaac King. Every man set his sights on her but it was

9

Duke Harrison, of all people, who was determined to make her his own.'

'Duke Harrison?' Susanna repeated as if the name should mean something to her, but she couldn't remember what. It was the way the woman had said it — she'd made it sound as though everyone should have heard of him.

'He's just about the richest man hereabouts. He was young and handsome in those days, too, and would have been a real catch, but that young lass had ideas of her own.

'She'd fallen for a ranch hand who worked for her father. She married him despite Duke's attentions and fine gifts. He was that angry, he had to be carried away by Isaac's men so as not to spoil her wedding day when she married the man she loved.'

'Did he get her in the end?' Lizzie asked, showing an interest in the story for the first time.

'That's certainly not the end of the story,' the old woman said sadly. 'If only it were. No, Elizabeth lived one side of town up at High Point and had three beautiful daughters, while Duke lived at the other side of town and had one son.

'It was said that Duke had never forgiven her for rejecting him and had refused to speak to her since then, but his son had fallen for her eldest daughter and behind his father's back, had asked her to marry him.'

The woman took a deep sigh and spat out some tobacco she'd been chewing.

'Well, just like her mother, the young girl had no wish to marry him and told him so,' Mary Franklin continued. 'The lad was heartbroken and told his father what had happened.

'Soon after, Elizabeth's homestead was burned to the ground. The poor woman, her devoted husband and their three lovely girls all perished. It was a sad day for us all, and even now the place still smells of smoke and the birds don't sing.'

'And was it the son that did it?' Susanna asked with wide eyes.

The woman looked around before lowering her voice.

'Most folks reckon it was old man Duke himself, but of course he said he was miles away and that he could prove it.'

'So it was the son?' Lizzie said.

'No-one could pin it on him, either,' Mary Franklin said. 'The judge had to declare it was just a tragic accident but I can tell you that's not what Ma and Isaac thought. They soon joined their daughter's family in the graveyard, I can tell you. The shock of it all aged them, all of a sudden like, and they were gone within the year.'

'Why would Duke do that?' Lizzie asked. 'I mean, what's the point in burning the place down? It didn't help him or his son get the girl they wanted. It just meant they all lost out.'

'Folks say he was just wild with anger and jealously and there's no telling what goes through a man's mind when he's that mad.'

'He sounds possessed by the devil to me,' Lizzie said. 'I think he ought to be locked up.'

'Lizzie, that's a wicked thing to say. I know we've never met the man, Mr Hamilton, and what he did, or probably had some hand in, was unforgivable, but it's not our business, and not for us to judge.'

'Forgive me,' Lizzie said, looking up at Susanna earnestly.

'Hush, now,' the old woman warned as she nodded to a couple who had just entered the general store. Lizzie had seen them outside the saloon when they had arrived. 'Afternoon, Connor. Afternoon, May. Your things are out the back, I'll get them.'

'Thank you, ma'am,' the gentleman called. He touched the brim of his hat and removed it with a little bow as he noticed Susanna and Lizzie standing near the counter. 'Good afternoon, ladies.'

'Good afternoon, sir,' Susanna said. 'Am I right in thinking you're Mr Hamilton?'

'Lord, no,' the man said with a laugh. 'Connor Riordan at your service,' he said and nodded to the two of them. 'Hamilton's my brother-in-law,' he explained, 'on account of him being married to my sister, May.'

At the mention of her name, the lady in question looked up from her browsing and gave a shy smile before looking back down at some lace.

'Here you are, Connor,' Mary Franklin said, returning with some sacks of corn. 'Hamilton's paid for them. He said you'd be in to collect on his behalf.'

'Thanks,' Connor said. He made to go and then paused before looking up at Lizzie. 'And she's right, you do look the spitting image of Miss Elizabeth, don't she, May?'

May glanced up nervously, nodded and looked away again.

'My name's Elizabeth, too,' Lizzie

said, smiling at Connor, then catching Susanna's eye and glancing down a moment before raising her eyes up to look into his. 'I'm Lizzie Holden and this is Susanna Newham. We're just here for the night before travelling on up the creek.'

'With your brother?' Connor asked.

'Jeremiah's my son and Miss Holden's fiancé,' Susanna said, empathising her last word.

'I'll be on my way, then,' Connor said with another grin. 'I'll load up the wagon, May. Will you be long?'

'I'll come now,' May replied and quickly she scurried after him, without making any purchases of her own.

Susanna looked at Lizzie who was now studying a piece of material with great interest.

'I think we've been out long enough,' she said.

'Yes,' Lizzie agreed. 'Let's go and see how Jeremiah is.'

'Is the young man unwell?' the old woman asked.

'He's full of cold,' Susanna explained. 'He's got a bit of a fever but nothing that a good sleep won't get rid of.'

'You won't be needing my grandma's special fever remedy then?' she asked with chuckle. 'It's guaranteed to cure the fever within a week.'

'He'll be fine,' Susanna said. 'Come along, Lizzie.'

Lizzie duly followed on behind as they headed back to the hotel. Outside, Connor swung the bags of corn into the back of the wagon, then rested his head on his arms a moment as he waited for his sister.

She appeared almost immediately and he automatically helped her up into the back of the wagon. As he did so, he noticed she flinched as he held her arm.

Susanna and Lizzie reached the door in time to witness what had happened.

'Are you hurt?' Connor asked gently. Her eyes looked frightened as she shook her head. Roughly he pulled up her sleeve but she was unmarked. 'You

16

can't be frightened of me, surely?' he asked looking quite hurt.

'Of course I'm not, Connor. What a silly thing to say.' She laughed a little but her eyes remained sad.

'Is that all you need?' he asked. She nodded again and silently he loosened the rope holding the horses and climbed up on to the front of the wagon, flicking the reins to get them moving.

Susanna and Lizzie exchanged a silent look but neither uttered a word. They returned to the hotel feeling refreshed from their little excursion, although troubled by what they'd seen.

★ ★ ★

Jeremiah was sleeping soundly. Susanna and Lizzie ate a beef stew in the back room of the hotel and then retired for an early night.

'I didn't thank you,' Susanna said as she got into her side of the bed.

'Thank me?' Lizzie asked in surprise.

'You saved us,' Susanna said, 'when we were attacked in the wagon. It all happened so quickly. One minute it was quiet and the next, all that shooting and the driver dead. You were so quick with that gun, I thought you were very brave and then to drive the wagon into town, all on your own. I simply don't know what we'd have done without you.'

'My pa taught me to drive a wagon,' Lizzie said. 'I know Jeremiah would have saved us but he was obviously sickening for something. He's not been himself today, has he?'

'He has been a bit on the quiet side,' Susanna agreed.

She didn't like to say to Lizzie that she thought it had more to do with the amount of alcohol he had consumed the night before than the fact he was really ill. He'd never been a good traveller and his way of coping, he'd told his mother, was to have a few whiskies beforehand.

'Goodnight. God bless,' Lizzie said as she hopped in the other side of the bed and pulled the covers up to her chin as she'd done since childhood.

It was pitch black in their room. It had been a cloudy day and there were no stars and even the moon seemed to be hidden. Lizzie lay there listening to the sound of Susanna's breathing as her companion slipped into a deep sleep.

Lizzie thought again of the tragic story they'd been told about today and wondered how much she really did look like the poor woman who'd died just because one man and his son didn't get what they wanted.

She thought too of the shy girl, May, who seemed so much in need of a friend. Eventually she slipped into a troubled sleep.

Jeremiah's Fever

The following day the sky was clear blue and the sun shone bright and warm, but Jeremiah's fever was much worse. He refused to get out of bed and wouldn't even speak to Lizzie.

'He'll be much better when he's slept it off and has had a good wash and shave,' Susanna told her. 'I think it is best we leave him here and go for a walk. It won't do us any good fussing round him. In fact that will only make him worse, and if we catch his fever, we'll be in no fit state to look after him, will we?'

'If you say so,' Lizzie said. 'I should very much like to explore the town a little more than we did yesterday.'

'I thought you might.'

'I wonder how far it is to High Point where the burned out house is,' she said aloud.

'Now don't go upsetting yourself about that old story,' Susanna warned.

'Morning again, ladies,' Connor Riordan said as he shook hands with Daniel, the hotel owner. 'I trust you slept well?'

'We slept very well, thank you,' Susanna told them both, 'but, unfortunately, my son is still too unwell to travel today. I wonder if our stay might be extended by a day or so?'

'Does he need the doc?' Daniel Bradley asked. 'He's just down the main street at the end.'

'Thank you, but sleep is a good cure,' Susanna continued confidently.

'The woman in the general store yesterday mentioned some medicine that her grandma made to cure people of fevers,' Lizzie suggested.

'That'll kill or cure all ailments.' The hotel owner laughed.

'Trust me,' Susanna said. 'Jeremiah's suffered for many years now but rest assured he'll be right as rain and ready to travel tomorrow.'

There was a brief pause while Daniel wrote something in his book.

'It's a beauty of a day,' Connor said as he adjusted his leather hat to shield his eyes from the sun. 'Have you ever visited this area before?'

'We're strangers to the place and we're just passing through,' Susanna explained, linking her arm possessively through Lizzie's.

'I was hoping to go and visit the burned out house at High Point,' Lizzie said. Susanna shot her a silencing glance but Lizzie continued.

'That story really saddened me yesterday and I couldn't sleep for ages for thinking about that poor family.' She paused. 'Do I really look like her?'

Connor made a point of examining Lizzie from all angles. He nodded.

'You've the same hair. She wore hers like that and yes, you have a look about you . . . the eyes, maybe,' he pondered. 'No, it's more than that. Yes,' he declared, 'you do look exactly like poor Elizabeth King, as was, and a bit like

22

her girls would have looked if only they'd been allowed to grow up like you, miss.'

'Now don't upset yourself,' Susanna warned.

'I could take you up there to High Point,' Connor offered. 'Both of you, of course. There's not much left of the house but the views of the valley are worth the trek. It might help you put the story behind you. After all, it's not as though you knew the people concerned.'

'Oh, please,' Lizzie begged. 'I feel sure, once I've seen the place, it will help me understand, and forget the story — and it is such a beautiful day today.'

'If it's not out of your way, Mr Riordan, that would be very kind,' Susanna agreed, not knowing how else they would occupy the time. 'I have a little business to sort out first. Perhaps we could meet you in an hour?'

'Suits me,' Connor agreed. 'I'm just going down to the doc's. Do you want me to tell him about your son?'

'There won't be any need,' Susanna told him, 'but I do thank you for your concern.' She paused and then sent Lizzie to fetch her cape which she'd left in their room.

Lizzie would gladly have run up the old wooden stairs, but knew she had an hour to kill before they'd be riding out to High Point with Connor Riordan.

She wondered if his sister May would come along, too. If they were staying longer in Jacob's Creek she wondered if they would have become friends. Lizzie hoped they would.

May reminded her of a girl she'd known at school. The girl had one leg a little longer than the other and hobbled along as she walked. Several of the other children made fun of her and even pushed her about to see if she'd topple over.

Lizzie was having none of it and told them so. Unfortunately the child moved away soon after and they'd lost touch, but Lizzie had never forgotten her and prayed she'd found kindness in another school.

While Connor had been looking at Lizzie to see if there had been a likeness to Elizabeth, she had stared right back at him. She took in his thick, unruly hair, sparkling blue eyes and cheeky grin. He had a kindly face and she liked the gentle manner in which he'd addressed his sister.

Meanwhile, downstairs, Connor touched the brim of his hat to Susanna and disappeared down the main street on his way to the doctor's house.

'I'd like a word, if that's possible,' Susanna said to Daniel Bradley, the hotel's proprietor, 'In your office, if you don't mind.'

He stepped back and frowned.

'You ain't going to tell me this fever is spreading, is you?'

'I think you know perfectly well what ails my son. Was he down in the bar last night?'

The man shook his head but Susanna

wasn't convinced he hadn't been bribed to keep Jeremiah's secret or perhaps the owner just didn't recognise him as being her son. He certainly took after the late Mr Newham in looks as well as character — more's the pity, Susanna thought.

'If I were to offer you,' she paused and looked down at her purse, 'a generous sum not to serve my son anything to drink, I would really appreciate it.'

'I can't refuse a man his right,' the little chap declared. Susanna snapped her purse shut and turned as if to leave his office. 'But that's not to say I couldn't see to it that maybe, after he'd had a few, it were more water than whisky.'

'Perhaps you're in the habit of doing that anyway,' Susanna suggested. 'I'll have to take other measures.'

'Other measures?'

'Jeremiah is my son, my only son and his pa's dead and buried. He's all I've got left. The bottle killed his pa and I don't want my son being tempted into an early grave, too. Understand? The man's a fool and he'll end up spending all we have and where will that leave me and Miss Holden?' She paused.

'I'm sure you wouldn't want that burden on your shoulders, but just so you know, as my son's so ill with the fever, I am going to take it upon myself to take care of his money and I can assure you I won't be paying you for any drink he has had.'

At that moment the office door burst open and a middle-aged woman walked in. She took one look at the situation, smoothed down her skirts and smiled at Susanna.

'Mrs Newham, I trust there's no problem?'

'I think we understand each other.'

Susanna looked at Mr Bradley who looked very uncomfortable.

'Six barrels need unloading at the back,' the woman told him. He scurried off, relieved to get out of the office.

'Can I help?' the woman asked. 'I'm

Mrs Bradley, part owner of this establishment. Is it about the fight Jeremiah had last night?'

'The fight!'

'He'd had a fair bit to drink. I dare say he thought it best to sweat the fever out of him. He and the lads were arguing about something. Nothing important, if I remember correctly, but it all got out of hand.'

'Spare me the details,' Susanna said. 'I merely came to ask your husband if he'd refrain from serving alcohol to my son. I didn't realise he'd been fighting, too.'

'You know what men are like.'

'Unfortunately I do. He's just like the late Mr Newham,' Susanna said sadly. 'Does he owe you money?'

'He paid for his drinks at the bar. Nothing was broken so there's nothing outstanding. Rest assured I would tell you if there was.'

'He has no money left to pay you any more,' Susanna told the woman. 'I beg you to leave him alone, let him sleep it off and we'll be on our way first thing in the morning, I promise.'

'And what if he gets demanding?' Mrs Bradley asked. 'I don't want trouble in my saloon.'

'I'll make sure he's no trouble,' Susanna said, heading for the door.

She made her way to the general store, bought a small packet and returned to the hotel. Before making her way to her own room and to see Lizzie, she slipped into her son's room and gave him the sleeping powders which she'd purchased.

Quickly she removed his money bag and disappeared before he stirred.

'Lizzie, my dear, I have a little errand for you to do while I get myself ready.'

'Of course.'

'I want you to take this money bag to the bank. They are to look after it until the morning when we will collect it just before we leave. Do you understand?'

'I do, but will Jeremiah be well enough to travel?' Lizzie asked, showing her concern. 'I called in on him earlier and he didn't seem to know who I was. He was talking gibberish. I've never known anyone acting so strangely.'

'What did he say?' Susanna hesitated. 'The fever can give you the most peculiar nightmares. Now pop down to the bank quickly and I'll meet you outside with Mr Riordan in a few minutes.'

Lizzie's Errand

Lizzie pulled her cape around her shoulders and headed off for the bank which was on the opposite side of the road just along from the general store which she and Susanna had visited the previous evening.

There were a couple of horses tied up outside. As Lizzie approached she was deep in thought about Jeremiah and his fever. She and her family had always been in good health and she had never seen anyone so poorly and it troubled her.

Lizzie reached out her hand to push open the door to the bank when someone with longer arms came from behind.

'Allow me, miss,' Connor Riordan said as he went to open the door for her.

He paused. There was a lot of

commotion and noise going on inside the bank. Connor turned to Lizzie and shook his head.

'Go back to your room,' he told her but Lizzie remained where she stood.

'I can help,' she said. 'I'm handy with a gun.'

Without a moment's hesitation, Connor handed her the pistol he'd just reached for and armed himself with his spare.

'You go that side and I'll stay here,' he told her. 'We'll get them when they leave.'

Lizzie slipped back into the shadows as Connor did the same opposite her. The shouting continued inside for a few minutes and then everything went quiet.

They heard footsteps coming towards the door. Lizzie's heart pounded in her chest as she waited for the bank door to burst open.

Moments later two men dressed in dark clothes marched out of the bank carrying two bags of money each. Their guns were in their holsters and their hands were full of money bags.

'Hold it right there,' Connor said, clicking back the trigger on his own gun. 'Miss Holden, take their guns if you please.'

Lizzie did as she was asked and threw them to one side out of reach. The men had their hands up but refused to let go of the money.

Suddenly they were joined by the sheriff and his deputy who was riding by and noticed the scene outside the bank. They stopped to arrest the men just as the bank manager and some of the customers came out to see what was going on.

In no time at all the sheriff and his deputy had handcuffed the robbers and were taking them off to the town's jail, leaving Connor with the money bags to return to the bank manager.

'I'll be back shortly to hear what happened,' the sheriff told the bank staff and customers.

'Come on, let's get this back inside,'

Connor told the manager. Lizzie bent to lift one of the bags of money in order to carry it in but it was too heavy. 'Don't worry, we'll take it.'

Inside the bank, Lizzie was pleased to see no-one had been hurt although one lady was sitting down suffering from the shock of it all. Lizzie had heard no shots but had no idea what had been going on inside.

Connor helped the bank staff return the money to the safe and then carried out his transaction. He waited while Lizzie paid in the money Susanna had given her.

'They'll be a reward for you two,' the manager said. 'I keep saying we need a guard at the door. Perhaps they'll listen to me now.'

'Well, at least no-one was harmed,' Connor said and then looked at Lizzie. 'I wouldn't normally allow a woman to get involved but I saw the way you handled that wagon the other day and guessed you were no ordinary girl. We worked well as a team.'

'I was brought up on a farm. I think my father really wanted a son, so he treated me like a boy.'

'You did well. You kept your head when it mattered. Believe me, not all men can do that. Let me escort you back to the hotel. I dare say you'll need a drink to calm your nerves.'

'I'm fine, thank you,' Lizzie told him. 'I don't touch liquor, but I would be glad of your arm to steady me as I cross the road.'

Lizzie handed Connor his gun, pleased to give it back and relieved she hadn't needed to pull the trigger.

She linked her arm through Connor's and leaned on him a little as they walked back to the saloon. Her legs felt a little unstable, despite her brave actions and cool head.

'May I ask you not to mention this incident to Mrs Newham?' Lizzie began. 'No harm was done and I carried out the errand she asked me to do. She has a lot to worry about at the moment with Jeremiah being ill and I wouldn't want to burden her more.'

'No problem at all,' Connor replied. 'And in return I should like to ask you not to mention this to my sister. She, too, is of a nervous disposition and I wouldn't want her to feel anxious about using the bank in future.'

'We'll say no more about the matter then,' Lizzie said as she withdrew her arm from Connor's steady side. 'Thank you for being there, though. I don't know what would have happened if you had not been. Those men would almost certainly have got away and they would no doubt have taken my money, too, and then what would we have done?'

'No use worrying about what might have happened.'

'That's true, but thank you. I'll go and see if Mrs Newham is ready.'

Lizzie gave him a little curtsy and disappeared back into the hotel and up the rickety wooden stairs.

High Point

Connor Riordan had not been exaggerating the beauty of the views up at High Point.

'You can see for miles,' Lizzie declared in delight. 'I can see why they chose this place to build a house. It's so beautiful. In fact it's the perfect place for a homestead.'

'It's fertile land and a good vantage point, too,' Connor told her.

'But no-one's rebuilt the house,' Lizzie said in surprise.

'There's no-one left to do it. Elizabeth's family were all gone and her parents died soon after. She had no brothers and no other kin have turned up to claim it.'

'Can we go to the chapel now?' Lizzie asked. Connor looked over at Mrs Newham for her approval but she'd been very quiet during their journey.

'Is she all right?' Connor asked Lizzie, lowering his voice. 'Looks to me like there's something mighty big troubling her.'

'I'm sure she's just worried about Jeremiah,' Lizzie said but then looked over at her companion. 'Maybe you'll give me a minute,' she asked and went over to sit beside her.

'Is there something you're not telling me about Jeremiah's fever?' Lizzie asked innocently. 'He's going to be all right, isn't. he?'

'He'll be just fine,' Susanna said briskly. 'It's you I'm worried about.'

'Me!' Lizzie gasped in surprise. 'I'm as fit as a fiddle. Whatever makes you say such a silly thing? I've never had a day sick in my life and I'm not about to start now.'

Susanna Newham looked seriously at Lizzie and was just about to say something when one of the horses reared up, neighing loudly and in distress.

Connor leaped to his feet and

charged over to his horse, his gun ready in his hand.

A single shot echoed out over the valley but neither Lizzie nor Susanna could see a soul about.

'What is it?' Lizzie asked. 'I couldn't see anyone. Was someone trying to steal the horse?'

'Snake,' Connor said. 'Keep back.'

The horse reared up again. He had a frightened look in his eye and it took some minutes before Connor managed to calm the horse down.

'Miss Holden,' he said at last, 'I couldn't help notice when you came into town that you had a love of horses.'

'I have,' Lizzie said quietly. 'But I don't think I . . . '

'I just need you to hold the head so I can take a look at his foot. I need to know if he was bitten or just spooked.'

'I really don't think it's at all safe for Miss Holden to go anywhere near that wild animal.'

'It's all right,' Lizzie said, making her way toward the horse but steering well clear of the dead rattlesnake nearby.

Connor waited a few moments while Lizzie soothed and calmed the horse, stroking him and holding his reins. She spoke quietly to him in a reassuring voice as though she knew instinctively what to do.

Carefully, Connor knelt and gingerly inspected the horse's front leg. He didn't stay close by for long as the horse tried to rear up again, clearly still in distress.

'I think he's been bitten,' Connor announced. 'He needs treatment and to rest. You two go over to the chapel while I take him to my sister. They've got stables where I can leave him and get a fresh horse to take us back.'

'Mr Riordan, if you think you're going to abandon us here, in the middle of nowhere, you're not the man I thought you were!' Susanna Newham said, showing her strength of character once again.

'The horse needs treatment,' Connor repeated. 'Go over to the chapel, see what you want to see and I'll wait here, but we'll still have to call in at the Hamilton ranch for a change of horses.'

'I don't need to go to the chapel if that would help,' Lizzie offered.

'You go,' Connor told her. 'I'll settle the horse. I'll put on some coffee.' He looked at the older woman. 'You have my word I'll still be here when you come back. The chapel's only over there. Look, you can see the steeple from here.'

'Very well, Mr Riordan,' Susanna said. 'It seems we have no choice but to do as you suggest.'

Susanna and Lizzie walked the short distance from the burned out ruin to the chapel where Connor had told them that Elizabeth and her true love had married and all three of their daughters had been baptised and then, all too soon, buried.

Inside the chapel it was cool.

'I should like to say a brief prayer for the souls of the family,' Lizzie announced. 'I'll pray for Jeremiah's recovery, too,' she added.

Susanna nodded but didn't say a word, but she did kneel beside Lizzie in prayer.

The bright sun seemed even hotter when they emerged, a few minutes later, from the little chapel on the hill at High Point.

They glanced over in Connor's direction. He'd managed to light a fire and the coffee was brewing.

'I love looking at old gravestones,' Lizzie admitted. 'I always want to know what stories they could tell, if only they could speak.'

'That's not something I would want to encourage,' Susanna told her. 'Let's not linger here more than a minute longer than we need.'

At the rear of the chapel they found a group of seven simple stones. They represented Elizabeth, her husband, three daughters, and her ma and pa who died shortly afterwards.

'Look, the second daughter was called Louisa,' Lizzie exclaimed. 'I had a sister called Louisa and she'd have been about the same age, but she died of cholera. She was much older than me. I don't remember her well.'

'I'm sorry to hear that,' Susanna said. 'Now let's be making a move away from this tragic place.'

'Do you think the bodies are really there?' Lizzie said aloud, almost to herself.

'What a lot of questions you ask,' Susanna said. 'Isn't it enough that the poor family died?'

'I'm sorry. I wasn't thinking,' Lizzie said quickly. 'Forgive me?'

'Of course I forgive you,' Susanna said rather shortly. 'There is nothing to forgive and you don't need to keep asking for my forgiveness.'

'Coffee's ready,' Connor said as they approached and he poured the hot, black liquid into two tin mugs.

'Thank you, Mr Riordan,' Lizzie said as she accepted hers. 'It's most welcome. Is the horse all right now?'

'I've given him something to numb

his leg. It takes a while to kick in so he should get us to May's all right. It's not far.'

'Just so long as we get back to the hotel before dark,' Susanna said. 'I wouldn't want to cause Jeremiah any undue concern.'

'I'll have you back before sundown, don't you worry,' Connor said, reaching out to collect their empty coffee cups.

The journey wasn't long to Connor's sister's ranch but the poor horse had been given something by Connor to ease the pain and now the creature was stumbling around as if he were drunk. If Susanna hadn't been so anxious, Lizzie would have found the situation funny.

At the outskirts of the homestead, Connor dismounted and told the women to wait. He was just about to lead his own injured horse to the stables.

'Mr Riordan,' Susanna called. 'I'd really rather you didn't just leave us here.'

'Honestly, Mrs Newham, it's for the best,' Connor said as he continued to walk. 'You'll just have to trust me. I won't be long, ma'am.'

Lizzie watched as Connor led the drowsy animal to the stables. He was greeted by one of the farm hands. They chatted for a while before Connor turned and made it to the main house, no doubt to see his sister.

'And what have we got here?' a loud male voice said beside Lizzie, making her jump and cry out.

'Easy does it,' he said as two strong hands clasped her waist and pulled her down to the ground. Susanna Newham was treated the same and the women were marched toward the main building feeling more like prisoners than unexpected guests.

'Look what we found, boss,' the older of their two captors said.

'Not now, Reeves,' one man, who was sitting by the fire, said.

'Oh, no.' Connor groaned.

At this the man by the fire looked up

and was obviously surprised to see two handsome women on his doorstep.

'What the . . . ' he began and then stopped and stared. His face drained of colour and he fell back into his fireside chair. 'Lordy, Lord,' he declared. 'She's come back to haunt me.'

May rushed towards him but he roughly pushed her aside. She lost her balance and fell. Connor went to her aid and then approached the man, who now had his head in his hands.

'These are just two guests from Jacob's Creek. They're staying at the hotel but one of their group is sick with the fever and unfit to travel so I offered to take the ladies out for a bit of sightseeing,' Connor explained.

'I bet you did,' the man sneered, risking a second glance at Lizzie in particular. He stood up, grabbed the open whisky bottle from the table and took a few good swigs, before moving closer to get a better look at Lizzie.

Lizzie could smell the drink on his

breath as he came up close to her but she tried to pretend she was braver than she felt and hoped she didn't flinch. He lurched forward towards her but somehow Connor made his way between them. The man slumped at their feet as if in a dead faint.

'May, get him to bed, he's had too much to drink,' Connor ordered. He looked at the younger of the ranch hands. 'You help her,' he said.

It took both men to get Hamilton to his feet and drag him back to his chair by the fire.

'Come on,' Connor said to the women.

They practically ran back to the wagon. Connor helped himself to a fresh horse from his sister's stable, briefly patted his own horse and all three of them raced back towards the wagon and off to Jacob's Creek and away from the Hamilton ranch.

After a while their gallops slowed but no-one spoke. Lizzie's heart was still pounding, but with excitement, whereas she noticed her companion had gone pale.

'Do you have any water, Mr Riordan?' Lizzie asked.

They stopped while Connor offered Susanna his flask. The water was warm from the heat of the sun.

'Thank you,' Susanna whispered.

'Was that *the* Mr Hamilton?' Lizzie asked with wide eyes.

'That was Duke Hamilton's son, Elijah, known as Lija and to many as Liar.'

'Did you see that scar on his face?' Lizzie asked. 'It looked as though he'd been clawed by a bird. You could still see the blood on his chin as though it had only just happened.'

'You notice too much,' Connor muttered. 'Sometimes it's best not to say things aloud, just keep what you see to yourself.'

'How can you say that when he knocked your sister to the floor?' Lizzie exclaimed.

'You keep out of that,' Connor said in

a threatening voice. 'Don't think I didn't see that, too, but now wasn't the time to deal with it.'

'We could go back for her,' she offered.

'Lizzie! Mr Riordan has asked us to keep out of his affairs and I suggest that's exactly what we do.'

'But that poor woman,' Lizzie continued.

'Enough,' Connor said as he jerked the reins making his horse speed up and it was all Lizzie and Susanna could do to keep upright in the back of the cart.

Back at Jacob's Creek, Connor seemed to be very keen to be rid of them as soon as they reached the hotel. He gave the briefest of nods and was off back down the main street. They didn't even have the opportunity to thank him for taking them.

A Few Home Truths

Lizzie helped Susanna to their room and fetched her a damp flannel to refresh her.

'Can I get you something to eat?' Lizzie asked. 'Mrs Bradley says there's some more beef stew if you want it.'

'I'm not hungry,' Susanna said. 'All I want to do is sleep.'

'I'll just make sure you're comfortable and then I'll go and check on Jeremiah. With a bit of luck he'll be feeling much better and we can leave this dreadful place.'

Susanna made to lie back down on her bed and then sat up bolt upright.

'No!' she called out. 'You can't go in on Jeremiah. I'm his mother. I'll do that and then I'll turn in for the night and I suggest you do the same. It'll be a long day of travelling tomorrow and you'll need your strength.'

With that, Susanna took a deep breath and walked across their shared room to the door. Lizzie could hear as she walked along the corridor to Jeremiah's room. She heard the knock and then, almost immediately the door opening and closing.

Lizzie sat on the end of the bed, waiting for news of Jeremiah. She expected Susanna to return quickly as the day's events had obviously taken a lot out of her.

After a few minutes Lizzie slipped off the bed and went to the door. She opened it and looked down the corridor but all the doors remained closed.

She waited for what seemed like ages and then, as she heard the piano music coming from downstairs in the saloon, she closed the door and wandered across to the window to look out over the street to see if anything was going on.

The sun was setting and the sky looked full of fire. She watched as the clouds made shapes above her. She saw a wispy snake-shape which changed into a gun. She saw a cloud looking like a rabbit with two distinct ears, then, as it faded and the darkness crept in, so she became aware of the moon and later the stars.

Lizzie had no idea how long she'd been standing at the window. The click of the bedroom door being opened made her jump.

'What are you doing in the dark?' Susanna asked. 'I thought you'd be sound asleep by now.'

'I couldn't sleep until I knew how Jeremiah was. Is he recovered now?'

'I'm afraid to say he seems even worse.' Susanna let out a little sob. 'He didn't even recognise me at first. His own mother and he didn't know my voice.' Lizzie came over and comforted her companion.

'Is now the time to call the doctor?' Lizzie asked. 'Or maybe purchase the special mixture from the general store?'

'He's sleeping soundly now,' Susanna

said. 'I really don't want to disturb him, but if he's still bad in the morning then we'll need to see what the doctor suggests.'

'So you don't think we'll be leaving in the morning?' Lizzie asked in surprise. Susanna shook her head. She took Lizzie by the hand and led her to a chair.

'There's something I need to tell you,' Susanna began. 'It pains me to say this but I shall never forgive myself if I keep quiet and I believe you have a right to know what you could be letting yourself in for.'

'Whatever do you mean?' Lizzie asked, her eyes wide open again.

'Unfortunately, Jeremiah takes after his father, the late Mr Newham. Now, believe me, Mr Newham could be the most gentle and affectionate man ever born but he had one weakness, and that was the Demon Drink.'

'But Jeremiah doesn't drink much at all,' Lizzie exclaimed as she thought back to Elijah Hamilton and how he'd behaved while under the influence of whisky.

'I had hoped to save Jeremiah and once he'd met you, I thought together we'd be good for him, but unbeknown to me he's started drinking. Maybe he's always done it and I was too blind to see, but it's definitely got worse and there are other things, too.

'He sometimes plays poker and loses more money than he gains. I have grown very fond of you and think of you already as my daughter-in-law and I . . . ' Susanna paused and looked away in shame. 'I wouldn't blame you if you were to decide to make your own way, once we get out of Jacob's Creek.'

'Leave you?' Lizzie squeaked. 'I don't understand what you're trying to tell me.'

'I know this is not what you want to hear,' Susanna said, standing and brushing down her skirts in a business-like fashion. 'At first I thought Jeremiah was drunk and that's why he was ill. I have reason to believe he's partaken of more alcohol since we've been here and that may have made him worse, but now I believe he really is ill.'

'I don't know what to say.'

'I realise I've been a proud and rather foolish mother. I've been trying to pretend he's something he's not. Believe me, as soon as he's better, I shall be giving him a good talking to and telling him he's got a choice. Either he mends his evil ways and settles down or, if he chooses the type of life he's been secretly living then, well, I shall have to disown him and I won't blame you if you do the same.'

'You wouldn't do that!' Lizzie exclaimed. 'He's your only son.'

'It's the last thing I want to do, I can assure you, but having lived with his wayward father for too many years, I know what's in store and I don't want any part of it.

'I am only telling you because I can see you've got a good head on your shoulders and, if you marry my son, you need to do that with your eyes wide open.'

'I don't know what to say,' Lizzie said again, looking down at her hands.

'Don't say anything now,' Susanna suggested. 'It's been a long and eventful day. We both need our sleep. Tomorrow is another day and hopefully it will bring us both some good news.' Susanna gave Lizzie a brief hug and then the two women prepared for bed.

Susanna was asleep almost as soon as her head touched the pillow but Lizzie lay awake going over the events of the day and what Susanna had revealed to her about the man she was about to marry.

Piano music drifted up from the saloon below and every now and again she could hear the sound of horses as men rode in or out of town. In the distance, she thought she heard a wolf cry out.

Lizzie tried to sleep but her mind was busy and no matter how long she closed her eyes and told herself to forget all her worries, she was still very much wide awake and alert.

What was troubling her most was the way Elijah Hamilton seemed to be treating his wife. Just as Lizzie had felt protective of her school friend, now she was keen to help Connor's sister, May.

Some time later, having still not slept, Lizzie slipped out of bed, dressed by the light of the moon and made her way silently out of the bedroom.

A Midnight Adventure

Lizzie turned away from Jeremiah's room and headed to the other end of the corridor and sat on the window ledge. With one neat scissor movement she moved her legs and long skirts from inside the hotel to the veranda which led around the outside of the building on the first floor.

Quietly she walked along the narrow wooden planks until she reached the back of the building where the deliveries arrived and found a wooden staircase leading to the ground floor at the side of the saloon.

She breathed in the cool night air and it soothed her, and she felt it might help her sleep.

It was dark but the moon was bright and Lizzie could see enough to make out where she was and where she wanted to be.

A muffled snort from a sleeping horse told her where the stables were. Quietly she crept across the yard and opened the stable door to find several horses.

It was warm inside but too dark to recognise which were the horses belonging to Jeremiah and his mother, so she stroked the horse nearest to her and, as quietly as she could, led him out of the stable and along a lane at the back of the hotel leading out of town and up the valley toward High Point where Connor had taken her earlier that day.

She led the horse for a while and then, when she felt it was safe, she led him to a pile of small, flat rocks and hoisted herself up on to the animal's back by standing on the top rock and climbing on.

She wasn't used to riding without a saddle but she'd done it before as a child. Besides, she thought, the road to the Hamilton ranch was not a long one.

The journey to High Point didn't

seem so far as Connor had stopped to show them various points of interest on their way. This time she used these landmarks to check her route and kept heading on.

It was true you could still smell burned wood and smoke at High Point and she smelled it before she even reached the spot of the ruined house, but at least she knew she was in the right place. Lizzie glanced briefly at the chapel opposite and then headed on, taking the road to the Hamilton ranch.

At this point Lizzie knew she only wanted to speak with May. She wanted to be sure the woman was all right. Lizzie had been unable to sleep and at one time she'd even considered asking Mrs Newham if they could ask May to accompany them, if she felt so inclined.

There were no gas lights shining and it was eerily quiet.

Lizzie dismounted and tied her horse to the outer fence, looking for landmarks to remember as she did so. She made good use of the shadows as she crept around the outskirts of the homestead before finally reaching the house from the side.

Her plan had been to walk once around the building in order to work out where the sleeping quarters were but the sound of heavy snoring came from one window and, as she looked round the front veranda she was able to recognise where she and Susanna had been taken inside.

Lizzie now realised she'd left it too late to call on May, unless the poor girl couldn't sleep, either. Instead she decided to leave her a note asking her to call in at the hotel and speak with her.

Lizzie removed her shoes and eased the front door open. She had expected it to be barred and would have climbed through an open window but instead, she was able to walk right through the front door.

She stood for a moment to let her eyes become accustomed to the light. The snoring continued to her left but something stirred and made a noise by the dying fire and she realised Elijah Hamilton was still sleeping in the chair.

Taking a deep breath she walked towards him, not really knowing exactly what she was going to say but knowing she had to make it clear that he wasn't to hurt May and that he needed to beg for God's forgiveness if he or his father had any part in the killing of Elizabeth and her family.

As she got a little closer to Elijah, he opened one eye. Lizzie froze. She'd left the front door ajar and a stream of moonlight made a shaft of light shine across the room lighting her up and giving her a ghostly glow.

Elijah closed his eyes tightly but not quickly enough. Lizzie had noticed his reaction and realised she'd caught him unawares. It was only now that she realised she was so close to the famous and dangerous Elijah Hamilton and she'd forgotten to take one of Jeremiah's guns.

She remained still but her eyes were

eagerly searching for a weapon or any implement with which to defend herself, should she need to.

Elijah opened his eyes again. Lizzie noticed his hand was shaking and he looked ghostly white himself. He stared at her for and then purposefully closed his eyes tightly and gave himself a little shake.

Lizzie had been so frightened and realised in one awful moment what danger she'd put herself in, that as soon as he'd closed his eyes, she turned and fled, closing the door quietly and picking up her boots.

She ran barefoot to the waiting horse, put on her boots, climbed the fence and on to the horse's back, urging him on as soon as she felt his warm body beneath her. She rode and rode until she was passed High Point and headed back to Jacob's Creek and the hotel. What had she been thinking of?

Lizzie retraced her steps, letting the horse back into the stable and making her way up the back staircase to the veranda, in through the window and along the corridor to her room.

Susanna was still sleeping soundly and she had no reason to think she'd been missed. It was only as she lay in bed feeling warm and safe that she realised how stupid she'd been. In no time at all she drifted off into a deep sleep.

An Extended Stay

The following morning, Jeremiah's fever had got worse and the doctor was called. She and Susanna took it in turns to mop his fevered brow. They said little to each other, both anxious for Jeremiah's well-being.

On one occasion as Lizzie had gone down to the kitchen to ask if she and Susanna could have a little broth, she was sure she overheard a man telling a story about Elijah Hamilton seeing ghosts and wanting the reverend to visit him so he could repent of his evil ways.

'It'll take more than a ghost to make a good man of Elijah Hamilton,' one woman said.

'You didn't see his face,' the man's voice said. 'I swear the man's aged overnight. He looks more like his father than ever before. In fact, if it wasn't for that fresh scar on his cheek, I would have sworn it was Duke Hamilton himself.'

'Serves him right,' the woman said. 'The way he treats poor May Riordan, he deserves everything he gets.'

'It seems May's taken flowers up to the chapel to put on the graves of Elizabeth and her daughters. The old man was crazy, but too scared to go up there himself and stop her.'

At this point they seemed to notice Lizzie standing in the doorway.

'Can I help you, miss?'

'I wondered if Mrs Newham and I might have a bowl of broth each. We've been looking after Mr Newham.'

'And how is the young man?' the woman asked as she fetched a ladle. 'Is he showing any signs of recovery?'

'I'm afraid not,' Lizzie admitted as she tried to conceal a yawn. 'I'm sorry. I didn't get much sleep last night for worrying about him.'

'There's no point in you and Mrs Newham making yourself sick over him, too.'

'The doctor says if we can keep him cool, he'll have a good chance of making a full recovery, but Jeremiah still seems to be burning up.'

'You have your broth down here, honey,' the woman said, setting a bowl and spoon down at the table and shooing the man out of the kitchen. 'Once you've had yours you can get the other woman down here and I'll give her some, and she can have a break too.'

'Thank you,' Lizzie said as she sank thankfully into the chair and hungrily tucked into the chicken broth and bread.

Jeremiah's fever cooled from a blacksmith's furnace to a simmering pot. Both Susanna and Lizzie were exhausted. Susanna had insisted that she would sit with him during the night and when Lizzie looked in on her she was asleep by his side.

Jeremiah was sleeping, his breathing rattled like the snake Connor had shot the previous day, but he didn't seem to be sweating as much as he had been. Lizzie took this as a good sign and closed the door. She returned to her bed and tried to sleep. She did doze a little, but woke up thinking of snakes.

She'd lost track of time when she was disturbed by Susanna coming in to bed.

'Shall I sit with him tonight?' Lizzie asked, seeing how utterly exhausted her companion was. 'I'm happy to do my bit.'

'You're a good and compassionate girl,' Susanna replied with a tired smile. 'But the doctor's given him some medicine which will make him sleep so we can both rest, too. Even when he wakes in the morning he's going to be so weak.'

Lizzie gave Susanna time to settle and to drift into a fitful sleep, leaving Lizzie wide awake and ready for action. This time she had more purpose about her and the feeling of this harmless revenge took her mind off poor Jeremiah, the unhappy-looking May,

68

and the tragic story of Elizabeth King.

Once again, when all was quiet in the saloon, Lizzie slipped out of bed, dressed and crept along the corridor, away from Jeremiah's room and out of the window, along the veranda, holding close to the wall of the building until she was able to make her way down the steps and head for the stable.

The moon was full and bright, although the stables were dark and warm. She was pleased to note their horses were being well looked after.

Lizzie was sure the horse must have recognised her because he rose as she entered and followed her happily out of the stable, along the lane and out toward the hills. This time she felt more prepared. She'd taken a carrot from the kitchen for the horse and Jeremiah's gun.

Even in the moonlight the journey was beginning to look all too familiar as she rode through the scrub-land out to High Point. Again she smelled the burned ashes before she arrived at the

69

bleak ruin of the house and the chapel opposite.

Once more she continued on to the Hamilton ranch, tied up the horse near the fence and crept again towards the house. She suspected that, scared though he was, Elijah Hamilton might be waiting for her tonight. She knew he might be armed.

It was only now that she began to question her actions. It had seemed so obvious when she'd been half asleep back at the hotel, but now she was here she wasn't sure if it was to speak with May or to give Elijah another fright to make him change his ways.

This time, however, she prised open the front door and then, giving it a little push, she let it swing open, creaking on its hinges. Meanwhile she raced to the end of the veranda and crouched down, out of sight but where she could see what was going on.

Sure enough, a few moments later, Elijah appeared at the door with his rifle. He looked left and right a couple

70

of times and then, on hearing a noise from the back of the house, turned, closing the front door.

Once Lizzie had caught sight of Elijah, she'd moved to the rear of the house and prised open a window which let in a draught, blowing out a candle and causing a rocking chair to creak as it rocked back and forth eerily by the fireplace.

Elijah, as she imagined, had gone to investigate and while he was doing that she slipped inside the house, grabbed the nearest thing to her, which happened to be a pair of old boots. She placed them outside the front door and left the door wide open again.

As he appeared again at the door, he almost tripped over the boots. She saw him scratch his head as he tried to understand what was going on. Then, as if she'd planned it, a wolf howled somewhere out on the scrub-land. Its eerie, melancholy song whistled on the wind.

Lizzie heard the door being shut,

bolted and the sound of furniture, a dresser or a table being dragged in front of it. She decided she'd unsettled him enough and, after a few minutes to check all was quiet, she crept along the shadows back to her horse, thankful she hadn't come face to face with Elijah again.

Caught Out

As she rode swiftly back to Jacob's Creek her heart was racing with excitement. She hoped she taught the cruel man a lesson and hadn't even fired a shot. Lizzie was so pleased with herself she didn't notice the movement in the scrub just as she reached the rocks where she dismounted.

No sooner had her feet touched the ground when she felt a gloved hand over her mouth and another arm around her waist.

'Don't scream,' a vaguely familiar voice said.

Lizzie had been taken by surprise but now all her senses were alert. She tried to think where she knew the voice, but just as she realised it was Connor's, he turned her gently round to face him.

'And what might you be doing at this

time of night?' he asked with a broad grin.

'It's got nothing to do with you,' Lizzie told him as she tried to pull away from him.

'One kiss and I'll not say a word, I promise.'

Lizzie hesitated. She knew she'd have a lot of questions to answer if anyone else found out, and she'd hate to embarrass Mrs Newham, so she stood on tip toes and planted a brief kiss on Connor's unshaven cheek.

'Oh, you're scratchy,' she said.

'My lips are softer,' Connor told her, leaning forward and pulling her into his arms. His warm lips descended on hers and were indeed softer than his rough cheek. 'Was that better?' he asked with a smile.

Lizzie's heart was now racing far more than it had done earlier when she'd been up at the Hamilton ranch. What was more, her knees had gone weak and she stumbled. Connor caught her.

'How did you get out?' he whispered.

'Out of the window and down the back staircase,' Lizzie told him.

Connor walked alongside her as they crept toward the rear entrance of the hotel. All was quiet. There was an atmosphere between them like when there's lightning before a storm. Lizzie guessed Connor was keen to know what she'd been up to, but she wasn't giving anything away.

Lizzie returned the horse to the stable and made sure it had hay, water and the carrot she'd taken. Then, just as she was about to leave, she found Connor as her look-out at the stable door. He gestured to her to be quiet.

Outside she could hear a man and woman laughing together. They sounded as though they had both had too much to drink. The woman was giggling as the man tried to pull her into his arms and kiss her, much as Connor had just done.

Lizzie stared in disbelief at the couple. The man was now cradling the woman in his arms telling her he loved her and how he wanted to marry her.

'Clara,' the man murmured. 'Marry me?'

'Ask me again in the morning, when you're sober,' the woman told him as she staggered back a little only to be drawn back into his embrace.

Lizzie felt Connor's arm on hers as he tried to steer her away. The couple only had eyes for each other and were making enough noise to mask their footsteps.

Lizzie couldn't take her eyes off them, but Connor almost pushed her unceremoniously up the wooden stairs into the shadows at the top.

'Keep going,' he whispered.

Lizzie crept along the wooden boards, neatly sat on the window ledge, swung her legs over from the outside back into the corridor and silently made her way along the hallway. At her own door she hesitated and looked down the hall towards Jeremiah's room at the end, wondering if he was still sound asleep. She remembered what Mrs Newham had told her about the doctor's medicine, so she turned away leaving him in peace and eased the door open to her own room.

She was relieved to find Susanna sound asleep and on her side facing away from her. It didn't take long for Lizzie to slip off her dress and undergarments and slip into the warm bed.

It was only then that she realised how her lips were tingling and wondered what Connor Riordan would think of her and her night-time escapades. Perhaps he would think she was no better than those traitors Duke and Elijah Hamilton.

She tried to come up with a plausible explanation for her being out so late on her own and with a borrowed horse, but fell asleep before she came up with a good excuse.

* * *

Lizzie was pleased she'd been allowed to sleep in and when she did wake, she awoke refreshed. As she dressed and combed her hair, she decided she would need to have strong words with Jeremiah Newham once he was fully recovered. As much as she cared for him and his mother she knew she didn't want to saddle herself with a no-good drunkard.

Yesterday when Susanna had kindly warned her that he wasn't exactly what she thought, she had been of a mind to forgive and forget, believing she could help him see the error of his ways and make a better man of him. That was yesterday.

Lizzie pinned up her hair and splashed a little water on her face from the jug in her room.

Just as she was about to pull on her boots she noticed how very dusty they were and took a few minutes to use the last of the water to clean off the evidence of her night-time prowl. Then, once that had been dealt with, she marched off down the corridor, prepared to do battle with Jeremiah Newham if he had made a miraculous recovery.

Susanna was mopping his brow and weeping as Lizzie knocked on the door and then gently pushed it open. To Lizzie's surprise Jeremiah looked pale, thin and weak, too weak to be anything but saintly. Again she wondered if she had it in her heart to forgive and forget his past indulgences if he were to promise never to touch a drop again.

'I thought he'd be better this morning,' Lizzie said, unable to take her eyes off the figure lying on the bed. His chest still rattled and every so often he coughed painfully.

'I think he's worse than ever,' Susanna admitted.

At that moment the bedroom door burst open and in stormed a very angry-looking Elijah Hamilton. He'd been followed by the bearded manager and a couple of his ranch hands including the man, Reeve, who had lifted Lizzie down from the wagon a few days ago and taken her and Susanna into the ranch when Connor was speaking with his sister.

'I want you out of here!' he yelled looking straight at Lizzie, then at Susanna and finally in Jeremiah's direction. 'Get out,' he shouted. 'And leave me alone.'

Daniel, the manager, and the two ranch men were able to restrain him and take him reluctantly down to the saloon to cool off.

Mrs Bradley appeared to smooth things over. She glared at her husband for allowing Elijah Hamilton and his men to disturb a sick guest and threaten his family.

'How is the patient?' she asked, although it was plain to see he was no better. She twisted her fingers and then explained that their rooms were needed and they'd have to move on.

'We can't move him,' Lizzie said. 'Look at him. Do you really think we want to remain in this horrible place any longer than is necessary with that bully around?'

'Lizzie, will you go and fetch the doctor again? Maybe it would be better for us to move him nearer to the doctor's place,' Susanna suggested in an effort to keep the peace.

Lizzie brushed past Mrs Bradley and made her way down the stairs to the reception area. There were doors to the saloon here and she could hear great guffaws of laughter as Elijah described the ghostly experiences of the previous night.

'It's true, I tell you. The place is haunted. I'm not sleeping there another night. I've told May, but she slept through the lot of it again.'

At that moment Connor came through the saloon batwing doors, almost bumping into Lizzie who'd paused to listen to Elijah's story. Connor smiled and then grinned as he seemed to make the link between Lizzie's night-time excursions and Elijah's ghostly visitor.

'Trust you slept well last night, Miss

Holden,' he said with a twinkle in his eyes, 'and that you had pleasant dreams of being kissed by a stranger.'

Elijah became aware of Connor talking to someone, or maybe he'd heard her name being mentioned. He charged at the open doors and again had to be restrained, though what he was intending to do to Lizzie no-one could guess. Lizzie could see the wild look in his eyes and shivered. She'd seen how brutal he'd been with his wife and she didn't want to end up another victim.

'Mr Riordan, I wonder if I could trouble you to accompany me to the doctor's?'

'My pleasure, Miss Holden,' Connor said, offering her his arm and shielding her from the angry Elijah Hamilton.

As they walked out of the hotel Lizzie froze at the entrance. Both she and Connor watched as the couple from the previous night were walking arm in arm toward the chapel. Lizzie looked up at Connor, who nodded.

'Come along, Miss Holden,' he said and steered her down the street.

'That was the woman we saw last night, wasn't it?' Lizzie whispered.

'I believe it was,' Connor agreed, looking serious. 'It seems they have a happy ending.'

'I'm glad someone has had some good news,' Lizzie told him.

'Is Mr Newham still unwell?' Connor asked. 'I did wonder, as you were heading for the doctor.'

'We were given to believe that if he slept well all night he'd be much better in the morning but he looks awful. In fact he seems worse than ever and I really don't know what to do. I'm sure either Mrs Newham or myself would have stayed with him if we felt we could have been of use.'

'You mean instead of wandering around the countryside in the dead of night?' Connor asked with a smile.

'I can explain,' Lizzie said defensively as she wafted away the reddening of her cheeks.

'Can you?' Connor chuckled. 'I told you, I've forgotten about the whole thing. Well, there is one thing I remember, and it kept me awake most of the night.'

'Have you got a problem sleeping, Riordan?' the doctor asked on hearing the tail end of their conversation. 'I can give you something for that.'

'I'm fine, thank you,' Connor said with a boyish grin. 'I've just brought Miss Holden to see you about Mr Newham. It appears he's taken a turn for the worse.'

Banished

The doctor came straight away to examine Jeremiah. Lizzie could tell by his reaction that he didn't like the look of him.

'Is it contagious?' Susanna asked. 'Mrs Bradley, the landlady, obviously thinks so and has asked us to leave. It looks like we're not good for business.'

'I can't rightly say if you'll catch it, but he don't look good.'

'Surely it's not safe to move him?' Lizzie asked, wondering where they could go if they were no longer welcome at the hotel. She didn't know of anywhere else in town that would have them.

'I don't think he'd know, or care, whether he stays here or slept under the stars,' the doctor told them. 'I hear it wasn't only the landlady who wants rid of you, but Elijah Hamilton, too. I can't imagine what you've done to upset him.'

'He seems a very angry man. I suspect it wouldn't take much to make him out of sorts,' Susanna said aloud. 'Now, what's to be done with my son?'

The doctor prescribed more medicine and complete rest and then left them to sort things out.

'Shall I go and reason with Mrs Bradley?' Lizzie suggested but Susanna shook her head.

'I have tried but she fears it will spread and in many ways I don't blame her. No-one wants to be around someone so poorly.'

'But you and I are fine. If anyone is going to be infected it would be us, and it hasn't happened yet.'

As if on cue, Susanna sneezed just as Jeremiah had done many times on the journey to Jacob's Creek.

'I'll speak with her,' Lizzie told Susanna. 'Don't you worry.'

Lizzie hurried back down the stairs in search of Mrs Bradley. Unfortunately she had gone to buy provisions at the general store and wouldn't be back for a while.

'Is everything all right?' a gentle voice asked as Lizzie turned to go back with no news for Susanna. Lizzie was delighted to see Connor's sister, May, standing in the doorway.

'I take it Mr Newham is no better?'

'He's worse than ever,' Lizzie said, 'and now the hotel managers don't want us here any more, and we've got nowhere to stay and Elijah . . . ' Lizzie just about stopped herself in time, realising that Elijah Hamilton was May's husband and she ought to be careful what she said.

'What's Elijah been doing now?' May asked, wringing her hands together.

'He also told us to leave,' Lizzie told May quietly. 'I was just coming to plead with Mrs Bradley to see if we could stay at least until Jeremiah is fit enough to travel. We were only supposed to be spending one night here.'

'I'll see what I can do,' May

promised. 'You get back to the patient and leave it with me.'

Lizzie watched as May turned round and headed back over the road towards the general store where she had just come from.

Lizzie hesitated a moment, not wanting to return to Mrs Newham without some good news but at least she now felt she wasn't quite so alone in this unwelcoming place.

It was good to feel that at least May was on her side and would put in a good word for them. She hoped that would be enough to lift Susanna's spirits as they were both in need of something positive.

Between the two of them, Susanna and Lizzie nursed Jeremiah, offering him sips of water when he was awake and soothing his fevered brow when he was asleep.

Later that day there was a gentle tap on their bedroom door as Lizzie was taking a few minutes to freshen up.

Cautiously Lizzie opened the door,

hoping it wasn't anyone else demanding they leave immediately. To her relief May stood there in her pale blue dress and bonnet.

'Connor has managed to negotiate another week and hopefully by then you'll all be fit and well and be ready to continue with your journey. Where are you heading?'

'A week?' Lizzie repeated, ignoring May's final question. She certainly hoped that would be enough and yet she was beginning to wonder whether they would ever be the same again.

'Thank you,' she said, remembering her manners. 'Please pass on our gratitude to your brother as well.'

'My brother has a meeting and will be a little while yet. I thought you might benefit from some fresh air. There is a beautiful meadow of flowers a short distance away. We could take a walk?'

Lizzie hesitated.

'I don't know if I should leave them.'

'Why don't you go and update Mrs Newham on the situation and tell her you can all stay at least another week so that it puts her mind at rest — and say that I've offered to show you that this town isn't all full of misery.'

'That's very kind of you.' Lizzie smiled. 'I must admit I won't be sorry to leave, although if I were to stay I would like to think we could have become friends.'

'I was hoping so, too,' May agreed. 'Go and speak with Mrs Newham and then hopefully she'll be happy for you to keep me company for an hour or so while Connor's at his meeting.'

'A week!' Susanna exclaimed, stroking her son's arm. 'I suppose that's better than nothing and believe me I shall not spend a moment longer here than I have to, but we can't move him yet. I fear it would be the end of him.'

'May has very kindly offered to show me a meadow of flowers. Can you spare me for a short while? I won't be long because I would like a nap before I relieve you again.'

'I think it would do you the world of

good. That's very kind of Mrs Hamilton to offer and I'm sure it will lift your spirits and you'can tell me all about it when you get back. It will do us both good to speak of something other than Jeremiah's fever and where we will sleep tonight.'

May was waiting at the end of the corridor. Together they walked down the stairs and hurried quickly past the saloon and out into the street.

'I love the colour of your dress,' Lizzie told her new friend. 'It reminds me of the sky on a summer's day.'

'Thank you. Elijah bought me the material over at the store and I made it myself. I have a little left. Perhaps I could make you a band for your hair?'

'Really?' Lizzie was touched by May's kindness and generosity. 'You'd do that for me?'

'Consider it done. I will get on with it as soon as Connor has taken me home this evening. The store has lots of lovely fabrics. Do you sew?'

'I can cook,' Lizzie told her as they

walked along past the forge and the old school house. 'But I've never been able to sew. Mrs Newham is a good dressmaker and she has offered to teach me.'

'I've noticed her clothes,' May said. 'She is a fine needlewoman and I love her lace collar.'

'She is very proud of that and wears it at every opportunity. For me, I'd be happier if I were a man and could wear men's clothes.'

'No!' May laughed. 'You can't be serious?'

'I was brought up on a farm by two lovely people. They'd lost their daughter, my sister Louisa, to cholera and I think they really would have liked me to have been a boy. So I learned how to shoot, ride a horse, round up the goats and mend all sorts of things. Mrs Newham would be horrified if she knew. I sometimes find it hard to be all ladylike, but I suppose now I have to get used to it.'

'Connor said you were a funny one,'

May told her mysteriously. 'I can see what he meant.' Lizzie turned away blushing again at the thought of that sensual kiss they'd shared.

She took a deep breath and silently told herself that kiss had only been her way to buy his promise to keep quiet about her night-time escapades. She was certainly not going to be calling on Elijah Hamilton again and there was never going to be a chance of kissing Connor ever again.

May was gazing out over a field of wild flowers. A billy goat was tethered in one corner, munching away at all the grass and flowers around him. Lizzie couldn't help wondering what it must be like to be married, as May was.

Silly though it sounded, Lizzie had given it very little thought, despite her engagement to Jeremiah Newham. He'd held her hand once or twice but he'd never been so bold as to kiss her.

The sun was shining and it warmed Lizzie's cheeks. May had been right, and this little walk had done her good.

The flowers did look splendid in the field — not that she was one for pretty flowers, she had always gone for more practical things.

'Come, let's sit a while,' May suggested and pointed to a stone wall where they could sit and enjoy the sunshine. Lizzie followed May and closed her eyes as she sat on the wall enjoying the warmth of the sun on her face.

'How did you meet Mr Newham?' May asked. 'Did his mother introduce you?'

Old Memories

May's question had taken Lizzie by surprise. She had almost forgotten what life had been like before she had begun her journey with Jeremiah and his mother.

It had been such a difficult year. The weather had been bad and the crops were not good. She knew her father, Bill Holden, was worried about whether they were going to have enough to feed them over the long winter months.

She knew, too, she had to keep this to herself as neither of them wanted to make Annie Holden anxious. She could be a worrier and would let even the slightest thing prey on her mind.

Sadly, her father slipped away in his sleep and not long after, Mrs Holden, being heart-broken, followed him a few months later.

Briefly Lizzie remembered the day

she died. Neither of them had been the same since the day Mr Holden had left them but this particular day would live in her memory for ever.

Mrs Holden had refused to get out of bed, which was unheard of. Usually she would be up baking bread and making strong coffee long before Lizzie got up.

Annie Holden dozed all day, refusing the soup Lizzie had made her. Then, just as the sun was going down she called Lizzie to her side and told her an amazing story.

Lizzie scrunched her eyes closed. She didn't want to think about that. It was all too painful.

'Have I asked an awkward question?' May said as she threaded daisies together to make a chain.

Lizzie jumped. She had almost forgotten her companion.

'Sorry, I was deep in my own thoughts. What was it you wanted to know?'

'I was just curious how you met Jeremiah Newham, that's all.'

There was something about the way she said his name that sounded as though she knew him, but as far as Lizzie knew, he had never set foot here before so she must have been mistaken.

Lizzie pulled herself together. She picked a couple of daisies and tried to copy May and make a daisy chain.

'Sadly I'd lost both my parents within a short space of time. We had a small farm but I couldn't run it on my own. When I was wondering what to do I overheard a man, who turned out to be Jeremiah, telling someone about his travels and how he was going to build himself a fine house on the proceeds of the money he'd made in the gold mines.'

'How exciting,' May said. She was all ears to Lizzie's story.

'It sounded such an adventure to be able to travel and to see different places. I'd never been further than the next village when we took cattle to market.'

'I've never been out of Jacob's Creek

but Connor has travelled quite a bit and I enjoy the stories he has to tell.'

Lizzie tried not to think too much about Connor — especially the softness of his lips.

'It all happened so quickly. One minute I was listening to this stranger telling stories about his future plans and the next he'd invited me to travel with him.

'Of course, I couldn't do that alone, so Mrs Newham came with us. We're to be married when we find a suitable place to live.'

'So you're not heading for anywhere in particular?'

'No, I don't think so but Jeremiah might have somewhere in mind.'

'What's happened to your farmhouse?'

'I sold it to the neighbouring farmer. He'd been after the extra land and his son was getting married so now they've got the farmhouse to live in. I'm glad because it was a lovely place to bring up a family.'

'And do you want a family?' May asked.

'Oh no, I'll be far too busy running the farm to be able to look after any children.'

'Running a farm?' May laughed. 'That's not a job for a woman.'

'It's all I know. I wouldn't want to be stuck inside all the time baking bread and preserving fruit. I'm happier outside planting crops and caring for the animals.'

'And Jeremiah, what does he do, apart from gold mining?'

'I . . . well, he's in business,' Lizzie said, slipping off the wall. 'I think it's time I got back to him and Mrs Newham. Thank you for showing me the meadow.'

★ ★ ★

Jeremiah's chesty cough got worse. He wheezed and rattled like an old man. More worrying was that Susanna Newham's sneezing was worse and she, too, had developed a nasty cough.

'It's no good,' Susanna told Lizzie a few days later, 'I think you need to leave us here.'

'Leave?'

'Yes. It's for the best. Either go back to where we came from or continue on and look for a more welcoming village. You have money from your farm. You'll be fine if you choose your ranch hands with care.'

'But I can't just leave you,' Lizzie told her, 'and I think Jeremiah has invested the proceeds of the sale.'

'Invested in what?' Susanna asked in surprise. 'What are you talking about, girl? That money was to be used to buy a new home for us all.'

'No, he was going to use his own money for that, but he said I could buy some land if I wanted, so I could have a smallholding of my own to run.'

'Jeremiah doesn't have any money of his own,' Susanna said slowly and carefully. 'We've been living on the small amount left to me by my husband.'

'But Jeremiah made a fortune in the gold mines.' Lizzie laughed, wondering how on earth his mother could have forgotten that.

'Gold mines?' Lizzie was now getting concerned by Susanna's worried look.

'He's never been anywhere near a gold mine,' Susanna said. 'He used to work in a bank but that didn't work out. I never did find out why.'

The following morning Lizzie went to relieve Susanna who had nursed her son all night.

'How is he?' Lizzie whispered. 'Did he get a good sleep?' They both looked at Jeremiah. He was paler than ever and his breathing sounded laboured and painful.

'I meant what I said about you moving on. Sad as I am to let you go, I do believe it's for the best.'

'How can you say that?' Lizzie asked, wondering if she had in some way offended Jeremiah's mother.

'I gave it a lot of thought during the long night. In hindsight I don't think it would be wise for you to travel alone. We've already been attacked once, it could happen again.

'I think we should find a suitable escort, perhaps someone who knows of a nearby town where you'd be made to feel more welcome.'

'I'm not afraid of staying,' Lizzie told her. 'In sickness and in health, so the vows go and I was expecting to become Jeremiah's bride very soon.'

'I insist and I don't think there is anything you can say to make me change my mind. I can see no point in both of us risking our lives to nurse Jeremiah. I am already showing signs of his illness . . . '

'Then let me stay and nurse you.'

'You're young and strong. My mind's made up.'

They were interrupted by a knock on the door. Lizzie stood up to answer it. To her surprise it was Connor, looking as tall and handsome as ever.

'Ah, good day, Mr Riordan,' Susanna said, as though she were expecting him.

'Lizzie, would you mind sitting with Jeremiah for a few minutes while I speak with Mr Riordan outside?'

'Of course not, but . . . '

'I shan't be long.'

With that, they disappeared. Lizzie heard their footsteps fade along the corridor.

Whatever could Susanna want to talk to him about, Lizzie wondered then she gulped. Had someone seen her and Connor share that kiss? All of a sudden it made sense. That was why she was being sent away.

Lizzie mopped Jeremiah's brow. He didn't stir.

'I meant well,' Lizzie told him. 'At first I only wanted to make sure that May was all right. I was worried about her. I didn't know Elijah would think I was a ghost and get scared. I know I shouldn't have played on that but I thought he deserved it. I meant no harm. I would never hurt anyone, you must know that.'

A gentle breeze cooled the room as

Lizzie rinsed out the muslin cloth she was using.

'I hope one day you'll forgive me and for then having to kiss Connor to make sure he didn't tell on me. Oh, what a mess!'

The Decision is Made

Before long Susanna returned and informed her that Connor Riordan, no less, was heading up the creek in two days' time and would accompany her as far as the Frontier. Along the way he'd show her each and every town in the hope she'd choose somewhere to settle.

It wasn't going to be easy, a young woman on her own with no menfolk to guide and protect her, but Connor had promised to do his best, despite telling her Jacob's Creek was by far the most resourceful place to be.

Susanna returned to Jeremiah, giving Lizzie time to take in this new information.

Lizzie lay fully clothed on the bed. She tried to sleep, thinking that she would offer to sit with Jeremiah while Susanna got some rest. As much as Lizzie tried to think about her future, it was the past conversation with Susanna that played on her mind.

What was it she had said about Jeremiah never having been in a gold mine? Surely there was some confusion. Perhaps she had misheard, or misunderstood? Lizzie was reminded she'd been told that Jeremiah didn't have any money of his own.

She shivered and got up to close the window. She kicked off her boots and wrapped a blanket around her. Her mind was in turmoil. Had her fiancé, the man she thought she was fond of, lied to her?

As Lizzie sat on the edge of the bed she thought about all the things she had learned from his mother. She tried to convince herself that it was Susanna Newham who was mistaken, but she'd grown to know Mrs Newham well and she trusted what she'd been told.

It gradually dawned on Lizzie that the man she thought she was to marry and whom she'd expected to spend the rest of her life with, had deceived her.

She had hoped that one day her fondness would turn to love for him and he for her but that wasn't ever going to happen now.

A few tears trickled down her face as she realised he was only ever after her money. She now suspected he had probably known she'd been left the farm and that she had no other relatives. Lizzie didn't feel bitter or angry, she was shocked by the whole story and hoped she'd wake up in the morning and find it was just a nasty dream.

There was so much Lizzie wanted to say to Mrs Newham before she left Jacob's Creek. She hadn't realised quite how important woman had become to her. Susanna Newham, rather than being her future mother-in-law, was certainly her friend, perhaps more like a kindly aunt or even an older sister.

Lizzie stared into the distance. She couldn't remember her sister Louisa. Lizzie shook her head as more unwanted, uninvited thoughts and memories came back into her head. She pictured her mother, Annie. Holden, on her death bed, holding her hand and telling her the most fantastical story that now sent shivers down her spine. Lizzie shivered again and went in search of Mrs Newham.

'I'm going to miss you so much,' Lizzie told her as she gave her a hug.

'And I you.'

★   ★   ★

The following morning Lizzie was touched to see a little crowd gathering as she left the hotel with her small bag containing all her possessions. The two horses were being left to be sold in order to pay the hotel bills, the doctor's fees and to make sure Mrs Newham was not left destitute.

On the boardwalk Mrs Newham pressed a parcel into her hands.

'I made this for you. It was for your wedding night.'

There was a moment's awkward pause between the two women. Lizzie was now beginning to feel anger and disappointment in being lied to by Jeremiah. Mrs Newham was clearly embarrassed by her son's behaviour. Fortunately, May stepped forward to lift the situation. She, too, handed Lizzie a small gift.

'It's the ribbons for your hair I promised I'd make for you,' she told her.

Lizzie looked down at the small parcel tied with a tiny pale blue ribbon the exact colour of May's dress.

'Thank you. I'll treasure these and think of you often.'

'Let's be going,' Connor said. 'No point in hanging around.'

* * *

Connor sat at the front of the wagon with his hands on the reins. He'd loaded Lizzie's meagre belongings in the back and was now waiting to offer her his hand to help her up to sit beside him.

'Can't you come with me?' Lizzie turned to the two women who had come to see her off. Mrs Bradley the landlady had also come to wish her well, as had Mary Franklin, the lady from the general store.

The quietness of the scene was disturbed by the noise of the saloon doors being forced open as someone was pushed through them and out on to the pavement. It was Elijah Hamilton and he wasn't happy. He didn't want to leave the bar and he certainly didn't like the fact that everyone had witnessed him being told to leave.

'Connor?' May called. 'Perhaps I could travel at least some of the way with Lizzie. We pass by the ranch. Could we not stop long enough for me to pack a few things?'

Connor studied his sister before helping her up to sit beside Lizzie. They rode off in a cloud of dust taking the road leading out of town. It didn't take

May very long at all to collect her belongings. Lizzie wondered whether they had already been packed, but surely she would never think of leaving Elijah. Despite his temper, May was devoted to him.

Connor whistled a tune as he guided the horses along the well-used track.

'He'll either not notice I've gone, or he'll miss me and be on his best behaviour,' May told them. 'It won't do him any harm to be left alone and he won't starve.'

Every so often the wagon would bounce over the uneven surface and the two of them would be thrown up into the air, often landing so close together they were almost touching.

Lizzie couldn't help being aware of the very masculine man sitting beside her. She was both relieved and disappointed that Connor kept his eyes on the road and hardly glanced in her direction until he decided it was time to stop to rest the horses and brew some coffee.

'We have an aunt in the next village. She married the preacher there. We can stay with her tonight,' Connor announced.

As they continued their journey Lizzie began to give some serious thought to what sort of place she was looking for. She wasn't sure whether it would be best to go for small and friendly or a large town where they would have a weekly market where perhaps she could sell goats' milk or goats' cheese if she decided on having a small herd on her farm as her father had done.

In due course they reached the preacher's house and were greeted by a friendly woman. She accommodated the ladies in the house but Connor slept under the wagon in their yard.

As Lizzie knelt by her bed and said her prayers at the end of the day she thought of Jeremiah and of Susanna and wondered how they both fared. She hoped that one day she'd be able to forgive Jeremiah for leading her on. She hoped one day to see Susanna again and to thank her for her kindness.

★ ★ ★

The following day they continued on their journey. It was a long day but eventually Connor found some shelter under a clump of trees and they made camp for the night. May and Lizzie collected wood for a fire while Connor saw to the horses.

It was cooler as they settled down to sleep. Lizzie was aware of the strange noises as she tried to drift off. Was that a prairie dog? Were there more snakes around?

Lizzie and May were huddled together in the back of the covered wagon. Meanwhile Connor had extinguished the fire and rolled up a blanket to use as a pillow and was dozing under the wagon.

It was a beautiful starry night. Lizzie remembered how her father had tried to point out the constellations. They all had exotic-sounding names but she couldn't recall what they were.

Suddenly Lizzie's senses were alert. She listened carefully and was sure she could hear voices. Next to her, May slept soundly.

Lizzie silently raised herself up on to one arm and tried to peer through the stitching in the canvas of the wagon. She was sure she'd seen something move outside and wondered if Connor was still below the wagon or whether perhaps he'd got up to stretch his legs.

Then she heard another voice. This time she was absolutely sure there were at least two men outside near their little camp. At this time of night they could only be up to no good. Lizzie wriggled down to the end of the wagon away from the voices.

Without a sound she slipped out of the wagon and then crouched down, partly to see where the intruders were, but also to see if Connor still slept beneath the wagon.

Connor had obviously heard something, too. Lizzie noticed him looking around. They both heard a rustle in one of the bushes in front of them. Neither of them moved. The noise had disappeared and then out of the bracken came a tall figure followed by a shorter, stockier one. They headed toward to wagon, clearly wanting to see what cargo she carried.

All Lizzie could think about was May sound asleep in the back, unaware of the potential danger she was in. Connor jumped up and surprised the men but there were two of them and only one of him. The men set upon him and tackled him to the ground. After a bit of a struggle, the taller of the two men mentioned a rope and they looked around for something to tie him up with.

'Hold it right there,' Lizzie said in her loudest, most confident voice. She tried to sound like her father when he had once caught poachers on his land. The two men heard the click of the trigger being pulled back into position. They stopped what they were doing and stared at her.

'I'm going to count to five before I fire. You'd better hope you can run.' She laughed as they scrambled to their feet and disappeared off into the bush.

'Well done, partner,' Connor said as he put out his palm in order for her to return his gun which she'd picked up from the ground. 'I won't ask if you intended to use it.'

'Of course I did,' Lizzie told him confidently. She wasn't sure if that was true but thankfully it hadn't come to that.

'Do you think they'll come back?' she asked.

'What? And risk you shooting them? I don't think so. No, we'll be safe for tonight but we'll leave at the first light of dawn. It'll be safer that way.'

'Goodnight,' Lizzie whispered.

'Lizzie?' Connor called. 'No need to mention this. I don't want to frighten May.'

She looked up at Connor in the moonlight. There was a gentleness about him where his sister was concerned. Yes, he was big and strong but there was definitely a caring side to him that Lizzie guessed only a few people saw.

She nodded but in the morning there was no hiding the visit from the robbers from May. Unfortunately they had returned and helped themselves to several of their supplies and even Connor's boots.

He was clearly not at all happy that they'd been robbed and he'd lost his boots. There was no whistling that morning as he searched to see if they still had their kettle.

'There's no point in carrying on,' he told the girls when he'd searched the panniers that were left and he looked again at the empty wagon. 'How did they manage to do that without waking us?'

Lizzie knew she'd been really tired and guessed she'd fallen asleep almost as soon as her head touched her makeshift pillow.

'They've taken the kettle and the water bottle. We'll have to go back. I can't ride for days without my boots.'

May and Lizzie exchanged a look. He did look funny padding around in his bare feet. Lizzie wanted to smile but Connor was busy throwing their few possessions in the back of the wagon ready to head off again back toward Jacob's Creek. Lizzie was relieved to see the gifts she had been given by Susanna and May were still in her bag.

'May, we'll go to your place first. There must be some boots up there I can wear. I can't go into town like this.' He looked down at his feet and wiggled his toes. Lizzie and May couldn't help laughing. Connor frowned for a moment and then joined them in their laughter.

'I'll be a laughing stock if anyone finds out, so neither of you better breathe a word of this to anyone. Understand?'

Both Lizzie and May nodded and tried to look serious but couldn't help giggling as Connor danced a little jig in his bare feet.

'You're quite nimble on your feet,' she remarked.

'Keep that to yourself as well,' Connor warned. 'I don't want them calling me the dancing bear or anything.'

With the wagon loaded but empty stomachs they set off back in the direction of Jacob's Creek. Lizzie had wondered if she'd seen the last of the place but perhaps she was destined to return after all.

Tragic News

On returning to town they learned that Jeremiah had become so weak he had slipped away in his sleep.

'I should never have left him,' Lizzie said as the tears rolled down her face.

'There was nothing more we could have done,' Susanna told her. 'He had no strength left to fight anything. At least it was peaceful at the end.'

'I should have been there for you,' Lizzie said. Being away for only a short time had made her realise how much she had come to care for the older woman.

'Well, you're here now and that's a blessing,' Susanna told her. 'I was wondering how to get word to you.'

The ladies dressed in black within 24 hours, as was tradition, and spoke with the preacher about burying Jeremiah. The whole of Jacob's Creek seemed to smell of the dye pot Mary Franklin used to dye their dresses. It wasn't a pleasant smell.

Lizzie did what she could to assist Susanna as she was not only grieving the loss of her son but struggling with a chesty cough and night fevers.

Connor and May offered their condolences. He had replaced his boots and provisions.

'I don't think I can make the journey now,' Lizzie told him when they met in the street. She'd been to the general store to run some errands for Mrs Newham.

'Oh, no, you've not gone down with the fever?' Connor sounded concerned and was looking closely at her.

'No. Rest assured, I am perfectly fine but poor Mrs Newham is no better and Mrs Bradley has asked us to leave the hotel by the end of the week. I was making enquiries at the general store but there is nowhere else for us to stay.'

'You're going to stay with her, then?'

'I cannot leave her. She's the closest

thing I've got to family and she's alone in the world, too. Thank you for offering me a lift but it will have to be just you and May this time.'

'May's deserted me, too.' Connor laughed. 'Elijah is on his best behaviour and she's forgiven him — again.'

'Forgiven him?' Lizzie asked but noticed a dark shadow cross Connor's handsome face. She realised it was best not to ask. He or May would share their secrets if they wanted to. 'I suppose I ought to return to Mrs Newham. She'll be wondering where I've got to.'

'There is a cabin just outside of town,' Connor began. 'It's more or less empty but I've kept it in good repair. If you must impose a quarantine on yourself, then at least take her there. No-one will bother you.'

Lizzie stopped in her tracks. She wanted to fling her arms around Connor who was offering to solve all her problems in one go.

'Thank you so much, that's wonderful and so kind of you.'

'Hold on a minute, lady,' Connor told her. 'I'm not offering you a palace. It's basic, but dry. You'll need to stock up.'

'I'll go at once and speak with Mrs Newham. How soon can we go?'

'I'm just going to pick up May and bring her into town. I wouldn't be surprised if she'd like to come with you and help you settle in.'

'That would be most kind,' Lizzie told him. 'I'll look out for your wagon.'

★ ★ ★

The cabin was barely a mile out of town. It was set back from the main track and looked deserted. Lizzie had been to the grocery store and bought provisions. Connor unloaded them and all their belongings from the hotel. May had kindly brought her some blankets to keep them warm at night.

May swept out the wooden shack and made up some makeshift beds. Susanna offered her help but collapsed on to the blankets at the first opportunity. Meanwhile Connor showed Lizzie a small stream. The water was cold but crystal clear and tasted wonderful.

'You'll not die of thirst,' he told her. 'I'll ride by every few days and check all is well.'

'Thank you both so much for all your help and for the blankets,' Lizzie said. 'I have something for you, Connor.' She handed him a pile of neatly folded clothes that had once belonged to Jeremiah. On top of the pile was a pair of relatively new boots. 'I hope these fit. There's quite a bit of life in them yet.'

'They'll come in mighty handy,' Connor said with a smile as he did a little jig to the wagon to load the clothing. 'Not a word, remember?'

'Don't worry, your secret's safe,' Lizzie told him. As she spoke she glanced up and caught his expression. He was smiling and they both knew he was remembering the time she had asked him to keep quiet about her creeping out to the Hamilton ranch at night.

'I have something for you too,' Lizzie said as she handed over a small chain to May. 'I believe it belonged to . . . my family.'

'I can't take this,' May said. 'It's far too important. You've got no-one left, you must hold on to this keepsake.'

'I shan't be wearing any pretty chains,' Lizzie told her. 'At least look after it and wear it. It'll look prettier around your neck with your lovely dresses.'

Lizzie waved off the brother and sister and — watched until the cart was out of sight. Everywhere seemed so very quiet now they'd gone. Inside the cabin, Susanna slept soundly.

Lizzie had a limited budget so she had only bought the bare essentials. She got out her little multi-purpose knife and began to prepare a vegetable broth which she was going to season with herbs from the general store.

Mary Franklin had suggested this

because the aroma might stir some hunger in poor Mrs Newham. She hadn't eaten in days but Lizzie was determined to try to tempt her to eat.

'Come on, try a little food,' she coaxed a little while later. 'We need to build up your strength. I don't want you to leave me here alone.'

'You should have gone when you had the chance,' Susanna told her.

'I did go, albeit reluctantly, but fate brought me back and now I'm here to look after you.'

Lizzie looked up. She thought she had heard a noise. It almost sounded like the soft fall of a footstep on the veranda. Putting down the bowl she cautiously went to the window and peered out. The sun was setting and the night was drawing in.

There wasn't a full moon tonight. Lizzie thought she caught sight of a shadow in the distance, but she couldn't be sure and didn't want to worry Mrs Newham.

She waited a little while longer at the

window but all was quiet. Perhaps she had imagined it. Just to be sure, she quietly opened the door. To her surprise there was a basket of food on the doorstep.

She stared. If May or Connor had left it, surely they would have knocked and come in or at least checked they were still all right. So who would have done such a kindness?

'Look, someone has left us a gift,' she said as she turned back to Mrs Newham. 'There's some bread and some bacon.'

Lizzie was delighted to see Mrs Newham look up and smile.

'Perhaps this place is more welcoming than we first thought.'

Time to Reflect

Over the next few weeks, Lizzie got into a routine. She'd rise early and fetch fresh water from the stream. She'd mix a small amount of oats with water and boil them over the fire.

Mrs Newham slept most of the time but Lizzie made sure she had several small meals each day and believed the woman was getting stronger.

Occasionally a carriage or horses would pass by but this was a small track and not the main thoroughfare up to High Point or to the canyon. It wasn't unusual for a whole day to go past without Lizzie speaking to anyone. She did, of course, whisper words of encouragement to Mrs Newham but more often than not she didn't receive a reply.

To pass the time Lizzie was beginning to cultivate a little garden. She didn't know how long they would be living there but Connor had said she had a free hand. On one occasion he had even brought her a small packet of seeds which she planted and watered with great care.

The evenings were the most difficult times. It was then she longed for a bit of company, for someone to talk to. She tried not to think about the fact that Jeremiah had got a fever and died and now his mother was ill. Was she going to be next?

Lizzie told herself she wasn't afraid. She had always tried to be a good person. She now regretted playing her prank on Elijah Hamilton which had led to being found on the way back by Connor.

He had surprised her and caught her off guard when he had asked her for a kiss to keep her secret. Over and over she relived those few minutes.

She had given him a quick peck on the cheek which she had hoped would have been enough but no, it seemed not. Connor had kissed her properly. It was more like a kiss a husband would give a wife, Lizzie thought.

She tried to banish any more thoughts of Connor, especially just before she went to sleep but so often he crept back into her mind and she found she was often thinking of him and wondering, hoping even, that she would see him again soon.

Just when Lizzie began to find herself talking to the kettle or to herself Connor came to visit and he wasn't alone.

'I've brought you these,' he told her. In his hand were a couple of ropes. On the end were two small goats, one male and one female. 'You'll have to keep them tethered but they'll soon let you know if anything's about.'

Lizzie beamed and instantly made a fuss of the two creatures.

'Now don't spoil them,' Connor told her. 'They're here to earn their living.'

He tied them up securely while Lizzie

fetched a bucket of water. At least now, she thought to herself, I will have something to talk to.

Mrs Newham was slowly gaining strength. She would now sit out on the veranda and watch as Lizzie tilled the soil in their little garden. The goats were young and a great source of amusement to both women and gave them something else to talk about.

As the weeks went on Mrs Newham felt up to doing a bit of sewing — it had always been a passion of hers. There was some mending to do and that got her started.

Lizzie was delighted, and felt it a real turning point but she was disappointed to find it only caused another problem.

'I shall need to go to the general store and choose some material. You and I can't stay in these black dresses for ever.'

Lizzie glanced over at her companion. It was good to hear her words but did she really think she was strong enough to walk into the town and look at fabric? It would be a long journey back and they would have things to carry which would slow them up. Neither of the goats was big enough to carry a load, nor were they large enough to hitch up to a little cart. It would be really useful when they grew a bit more.

'You could choose for me or ask Mrs Franklin to help. She was always very helpful.'

Lizzie looked over at Mrs Newham. She clearly had no idea that they were both still shunned from the town. People continued to fear they would bring a fever with them.

They had made do with what provisions they had brought with them. Strangers had been kind and left the occasional loaf of bread or preserves. Connor called round now and again and always gave them food.

'Don't you worry about catching our fever?' Lizzie had once asked him.

'I think you and I would be ill already

if we were going to get it. I'll take my chance.'

Lizzie hoped he was right.

'And how is May?' she asked. May had only visited once or twice in secret. It seemed she too would be cast out by the townsfolk if they knew she was in contact with them. Lizzie always made sure she kept her distance from her friend and prayed she would not pass on any fever.

'Unfortunately that husband of hers is up to his cruel old tricks, calling her names,' Connor told her. 'I'd welcome the chance to shoot him if I could.'

'Connor! That's a dreadful thing to say.'

'I beg your pardon, but no-one treats my sister badly and gets away with it.'

'Is that what happens?'

'I can't prove it and May is always quick to defend him. She says he's a good man most of the time and she loves him.'

'Well, you can tell her that Mrs Newham is getting much stronger. She no longer sleeps all day but is restless and wants to sew. She has started making a few small garments which we hope to sell in the spring.'

'I'll let her know,' he promised and then he was off, riding away into the distance on his horse.

'He and his sister have been good to us,' Susanna Newham said aloud.

'Lots of other people, too,' Lizzie told her. 'I wish I knew who it was who leaves us things, then I could thank them or do something in return.'

'One day we'll find out, I'm sure.'

Empty Pockets

'I thought perhaps, when May does come to visit us,' Mrs Newham began, 'if I gave her my specifications, perhaps she'd buy me fabric or describe to me what materials they have.'

Lizzie looked doubtful and concentrated on stirring the stew.

'What is it, girl? Do you think she, too, is avoiding us?'

Lizzie sighed. She picked up the bucket and headed off for the stream.

'What is it?' Mrs Newham asked on her return. 'There is something you're not telling me.'

Although she was reluctant to be the provider of bad news, it was a relief to be able to share the load.

'We have no money left,' Lizzie said again. 'I have made some goats' cheese and we can try to sell those garments you've made but I think people still believe we carry the fever.'

'So, what are we going to do?' Lizzie could hear the panic in her companion's voice.

'Connor hasn't been to visit for a while. Next time he comes, which I hope will be soon, I will ask him to take my jewellery and try to sell that.'

'You can't sell your keepsakes, that's all you've got left of your parents. You must keep those treasures.'

'And let us starve?'

Mrs Newham looked at the bare shelves and nodded. They had no choice.

Sure enough, Connor did call by the following day. He brought them bread and potatoes and agreed to take her chains and a watch of her father's to the pawnbroker in the next village.

'Mrs Bradley, the landlady from the hotel, was asking after you. I told her that Mrs Newham was getting stronger by the day and that you had never succumbed to the sickness. I am hoping she'll spread the word and then you'll be welcome back in town.'

'That would make such a difference,' Lizzie told him. 'It's so hard making ends meet when we have no way of selling the things we're producing.'

They showed Connor the children's clothes Mrs Newham had cleverly sewn out of their old clothes. Lizzie had whittled a few things with her knife and she'd found some berries and had made preserves.

'There's a pedlar called Thomas. I'll suggest he calls in to see your wares. Maybe he'll sell them on your behalf.'

'Can we trust him?'

'I would trust him with my life,' Connor assured her, 'and you can too.'

* * *

A few days later, Lizzie looked up as both the goats started to call out.

'It's May!' she said excitedly. 'I've missed her so much.'

The three of them sat sipping coffee on the veranda. May had been given a tour of the little garden and had been introduced to the goats.

Lizzie told May how they were indebted to her brother.

'Without him we would have starved.

'He told me you'd given him your jewellery to sell or to pawn. It's such a shame you have to do that.' May fiddled with the chain around her neck that Lizzie had given her to keep safely.

'I'm sure my . . . my mother would have done the same under the circumstances,' Lizzie told them but she couldn't help looking away.

'What's up, girl?' Mrs Newham asked. 'This happens every time you talk about your family. Isn't it about time you told us the truth?'

May and Susanna looked at Lizzie as she considered sharing her story. Lizzie nodded. Now was the time to include them in her secret.

'The day my mother passed away she told me an incredible story. At first I didn't believe it but the more I've thought about it and the more I've come to learn, I realise there is more than an element of truth in it.'

'What did she say?' May asked. 'And why leave it until her final breath?'

'She told me she and my father were not my true parents.' Lizzie's eyes filled with tears but she soldiered on. 'He and his wife took me in when I was a little girl. They lived a quiet life and no-one ever asked questions.'

'I remember you telling me you had a sister, Louise?'

'Louisa, yes — but she died of cholera. She was a lot older than me. I sometimes remember another girl, too, but I think she must be from a recurring dream.'

'So do you know who your real parents are?'

'My mother was very frail when she told me this story. All she really said was that I'd always been like a proper daughter to them and that they both had always felt blessed.'

May fiddled again with the chain around her neck.

'You said this had once belonged to your mother. Was it your real mother?'

'I've thought a lot about that, too, and I think it must have been. I can never recall Mr or Mrs Holden, my adoptive parents, ever wearing any finery. They were simple folk.'

'And now I suppose you'll never know the whole truth,' May said sadly.

'I'd love to know but there is no-one left to tell me now.'

'You must content yourself that you were loved and valued,' Susanna told her. 'That's all we can ever hope for.'

* * *

To Lizzie's surprise she had not one, but two unexpected visitors. Thomas the pedlar appeared at the door. He was short and sprightly with a white beard.

'I heard you had things to sell,' he told them. 'Riordan sent me.'

Susanna showed the pedlar the things she'd made. He seemed impressed enough to strike up a bargain with the women.

'I'll call in again when I'm passing through,' he told them, 'so you had better keep yourselves busy.'

'I've just baked some oatcakes,' Susanna told him. 'Won't you stay and join us for a hot drink? Or some ale?'

It was quite a jolly party that sat on the veranda that afternoon. Thomas the pedlar told them stories of his travels. He made them laugh and promised to call again whenever he was next in the area. Just as he was leaving he noticed the chain hanging around May's neck. He seemed dazzled by it.

'And where did you get such a pretty thing?' he asked. May shot a look at Lizzie. The pedlar looked a little more closely at the three women but if he was going to make some comment, he decided to keep it to himself.

'It was a gift,' May said, fiddling with the necklace hanging round her throat.

'And am I right in thinking you don't often wear it?'

'How on earth do you know that?' May said, taken completely by surprise. 'I only wear it on special occasions.'

'I'd keep it out of sight if I were you,' he said mysteriously and tapped the side of his nose. 'Best be off now. Look after yourselves.'

No sooner had the pedlar gone but May told them she too ought to make a move. She didn't want Elijah to ask too many questions as to where she had been all afternoon.

The little wooden cabin seemed very quiet once their visitors had gone.

Lizzie was pleased to note that for the first time she could remember, she was ready to go to bed earlier than Susanna. Lizzie smiled to herself, thinking that this really meant she was over the fever and stronger than ever.

Much to their surprise May returned the following day. She was wearing her pale blue dress again but Lizzie noticed today she wasn't wearing the chain she'd given her.

'Another visit?' Mrs Newham said.

'Are you after more of Lizzie's oat-cakes?'

'I was pleased to see you both so well. I think now is the time for all three of us to walk into town and to the general store together. Everyone needs to see you are fully recovered with no sign of the sickness. Only that way will they accept you back into the community.'

'She's right,' Susanna said.

'Can you make it to the town and back?' Lizzie asked.

'Of course I can,' Susanna replied indignantly. 'There's nothing wrong with me now.'

The three women strolled slowly up the road from the cabin and into the village. They turned heads as they passed people on their way but no-one said anything.

Lizzie took a deep breath as they entered the general store. She knew there was a real possibility that they could be asked to leave. She understood, knowing that no one wanted to run the risk of catching an illness from them.

They held their heads high and entered as though they did this every day of the week.

'Can I help you, ladies?' Mary Franklin greeted them with a warm smile. Susanna was keen to see the fabrics, as was May.

'We have no money for material,' Lizzie warned them as she placed an order for oats, candles, coffee and the basic food essentials.

'Nice to have you back,' Mary whispered. 'You've been sorely missed.'

Lizzie smiled but her face soon darkened when she looked up and saw both Elijah and Duke Hamilton looking down at her.

'I thought you were dead,' Duke said to Susanna and then turned to Lizzie. 'And I thought you'd run away.'

'We're back,' Lizzie said. 'And we're here to stay so you'd better get used to it.' Her words were bold and confident but inside, her heart was pounding like horses' hooves on dry ground.

Elijah took May with him back to their ranch. Duke followed along.

'I hear you're quite a dressmaker?' Mary asked. 'I used to do lots myself but my eyes aren't what they used to be. Are you able to do some alterations?'

'I'd love to,' Susanna said quickly. 'I can make garments, too.'

They discussed the dress that Susanna was wearing which she had made herself out of scraps of old material.

Lizzie made her purchases. She sat on the veranda waiting for Susanna to finish. She didn't want to admit it but the walk into the town after so long had actually taken more out of her than she would have expected. She was looking forward to getting back to the cabin and having an early night.

In the background she could hear Susanna chatting away and was pleased that it seemed they were now welcome back in the town, which was going to make their lives much easier.

As Lizzie waited, she thought about the first time they'd seen the general store when they had just arrived. It was on that occasion that everyone had stared at her and she'd learned about the tragic story of the family who'd been lost in the fire up at High Point.

Lizzie wandered back into the store. She and Susanna were now the only customers.

'Can you tell me more about the fire at High Point?' Lizzie asked. Mary was in one of her chatty moods and seemed more than happy to talk the afternoon away.

Again Lizzie heard that Duke Hamilton had fallen for a beautiful girl called Elizabeth King but she had chosen to marry someone else even though he was not nearly so rich as Duke. He took his anger out on everyone, so it was said, and he would pick fights with anyone and everyone.

Then, some years later Duke did marry. His wife produced one son, Elijah. He grew up and of all people he fell hopelessly in love with Elizabeth's eldest daughter. He, too, was rejected, which only went to fuel Duke's anger. Nothing could ever be proven. Maybe the fire was just some horrible accident. No-one could say how it started.

'And people say I look like the lady who died?' Lizzie asked again.

'You're the image of her.'

'And she had three daughters, didn't she? Connor took us up to the chapel to see the gravestones.'

'Now why would he want to do that?' The shopkeeper laughed.

'What were their names . . . I can't remember?'

'The oldest one was Martha, then Louisa only a year later. Those two were like twins, no-one could tell them apart. And then many years later, not long before the fire, they had another little girl. She was called Elizabeth after her mother. I think they would have liked a son to run the farm but it wasn't meant to be.'

Lizzie sat deep in thought as Susanna

examined every bit of fabric and every single ribbon on the premises.

Lizzie realised that if the story were true, May was not Elijah's first choice of wife and she wondered how she felt about that. May had asked her how she had met Jeremiah, but she had not had the opportunity to ask why May had agreed to marry Elijah.

She scrunched up her face as she tried to visualise both Elijah and Duke. Were they to be considered handsome men? Lizzie had to admit there was something about their dark looks which did have an appeal.

It was much later than they had intended when they eventually left the town and began their slow walk home. The sun was going down and there was a cooler nip in the air. Fall was fast approaching.

Much to their surprise there were two people waiting for them when they arrived back at the cabin. Lizzie was instantly on the defence but was relieved, as they got closer, to see that one of their visitors was Thomas the pedlar. He had an older man with him.

'This is Mr King. He used to live in the town until tragedy struck and he moved out.'

'Nice to meet you, Mr King,' Lizzie said. Lizzie and Susanna felt obliged to invite their guests in and offer them the last of the beef stew. Susanna heated it up while Lizzie fed the goats.

As they were serving up the food the older man reached out for Lizzie's hand and examined it as though he'd never seen a woman's hand before.

'And where do you come from?' he asked after a little while. 'You haven't always lived round here, have you?'

'No, we were just passing through when my fiancé, Mrs Newham's son, became ill and we were forced to change our plans.'

Lizzie and Susanna were pleased to have people call by but were relieved when it was time for them to go.

'I like Thomas the pedlar. His stories make me laugh.'

'What about this Mr King?' Lizzie asked. 'He asked so many questions and kept looking at me in such a strange way.'

'I didn't notice,' Susanna said. 'But that pedlar has nice eyes.'

Dreams or Nightmares?

That night Lizzie could not get to sleep. The moon was so bright it was almost daylight outside. Susanna seemed to have no trouble getting off to sleep. When Lizzie did eventually drift off she had a troubled night. Her dream was a mix of all the people she'd seen that day. There was Elijah and Duke Hamilton as well as Mr King whom she'd only just met.

She thought back to a time when she was just a little girl. Her parents were there but were they her real parents or Mr and Mrs Holden? Her sister was there, too, and another girl, but none of the characters was clear.

Lizzie woke early. She'd been thinking about the handsome Connor and wondering where he lived. No-one had ever said, not even May. She must have dozed again because when she did wake up properly the sun was high in the sky and Susanna was up, busy doing the chores.

'At least that tells me you're fully recovered.' Lizzie laughed. She was delighted to see Susanna in a pale green dress and not in her black mourning dress. She herself had stopped wearing black a little while ago when the dress had become impractical when working in the garden and she'd torn her skirts.

'I suppose we ought to be thinking of moving on.'

'Really? Do we have to? I rather like it here now. I haven't felt this settled in such a long time. It's good.'

'But Connor's only lent us this cabin on a temporary basis until you were recovered and we were out of quarantine. I don't know what he used to use it as, but he'll need it back.'

'But where can we go?'

'Are you sure Jeremiah didn't have any plans?'

'He had lots of plans but they were all in his head and I doubt they would have come to fruition. He was always a bit of a dreamer, wasn't he?'

'I don't think I ever got to know him that well,' Lizzie admitted.

'You seem rather quiet yourself today,' Susanna said. 'I hope you're not going down with anything.'

'I had several dreams last night which have disturbed me,' Lizzie confessed. 'It was all a bit muddled and I suppose that's the way it will stay but it has unsettled me. I suppose that's why I was thinking we ought to move on.'

'Hello!' a familiar voice called. May was hurrying down the path toward the cabin. 'Can I come in?'

May slipped through the door and almost hid in the corner as though she were being followed. She had an anxious look about her but would not confide in either of the ladies.

'Does Connor live with you?' Lizzie asked as she put a pan of coffee on to boil.

'No, he and Elijah barely speak to each other. I'm afraid he wouldn't be welcome at the Hamilton ranch, although Duke has been kinder of late.'

'Can you trust Duke?' Susanna asked. 'I mean, is he up to something?'

'I don't think so. He's a tired old man now and genuinely seems grateful for the little things I do for him.'

'And Elijah?'

'Well, he's a different matter. One minute he's gentle and attentive and the next moment he's . . . moody. I tend to avoid him if I can and keep my head down if he's around.'

Lizzie was about to respond but Susanna caught her eye and shook her head.

'So, where does Connor live?' Lizzie asked to change the subject. 'Reluctant though we are, Susanna and I are no longer living in quarantine and that was the deal, so really we ought to let him have his cabin back. We don't know what we'd have done without his kindness throughout this awful time.'

'He lives up on the hills. He'll be

fine. He'd let you know if he needed it back,' May told them.

Lizzie poured them all some hot coffee and slid an enamel mug to May.

'So now tell us how you met Elijah,' Lizzie urged, trying to keep the conversation light.

'It was years ago. Connor and I lost our parents. We had little money and both had to work to earn enough to feed ourselves. The doctor very kindly offered to have me as his assistant and said we could live in one of his outbuildings.'

'I didn't know that.'

'I used to make up mixtures for him and he taught me how to put a bandage on.'

'Is that how you met Elijah?'

'Yes. One day there was an awful dust storm. Everyone was rushing about like crazy. You couldn't see your hand in front of your face and people tried to take cover. The horses were scared and one must have reared up and kicked Elijah in the leg.'

'Ouch! I bet that hurt.'

'He was in a bad way. He lost a lot of blood but the doctor was good and stitched him up. I sat with him for hours and cared for him until he was strong again.'

'And he asked you to marry him?'

'He did and I accepted.' May looked at both her friends. 'I know he has a crue tongue and can be a bit boisterous but that leg still gives him pain and sometimes it makes him moody and he takes it out on whoever is nearby and often that is me.'

'But that's not fair! You looked after him.'

'I did then and I will continue to do so. In sickness and in health, remember?'

May only stayed a short while, saying she had to get back in to town before she was missed.

'I worry about that girl,' Susanna said, 'but at least I understand a bit more now.' Lizzie nodded in agreement. No more needed to be said.

Mystery Solved

Late one afternoon, Lizzie was collecting firewood when she heard Susanna speaking with someone.

Once again Thomas and Mr King had called by. Lizzie was surprised, because they only had a few things to sell that which they now kept in Jeremiah's old trunk.

Lizzie opened it up to show Thomas the pedlar what he might be interested in buying from them, but today he didn't show much interest at all.

'Sit down, girl, Mr King has some news for you,' Thomas told her. She wasn't used to be told to sit down in her own home but Thomas had a gentle voice so she did as she was asked. Susanna joined them at the wooden table.

'When I was here before . . . ' Mr King began. 'The other lady, the one in the blue dress?'

'That's May, she's our good friend.'

'And the necklace she wore, am I right in thinking you had given it to her?' Mr King was looking directly at Lizzie.

'Yes, she's been very kind to us both — as has her brother.'

'It was Connor who put us on to you in the first place,' he said mysteriously.

'What's my necklace got to do with Connor?' Lizzie asked.

She was not used to sitting down doing nothing, she was always busy fixing and mending the things about the place and hoped to return the little wooden cabin in a better state than when they'd first moved in. It was the least she could do to thank Connor for his generosity.

'My niece was Elizabeth King, the lass who died tragically all those years ago up at High Point. I take it you know the story?'

'We've heard about it, of course.'

'Word had reached me that a young

woman looking like Elizabeth had come in to town. I had to see you for myself and I can confirm you are so very like her, it warms my heart.'

'But I'm Lizzie Holden.'

'Hear me out,' Mr King continued. 'I recognised that necklace. I mentioned it to Connor who showed me others you'd given him to pawn. Incidentally, I've bought the lot from him, so make sure you get the money.'

'We can trust Connor Riordan,' Susanna said.

'All that jewellery belonged to my niece and her family. How did you come by it?'

Lizzie took a deep gulp.

'The woman I always thought was my mother, Annie Holden, gave it to me saying it was mine to treasure. I didn't question it. I only learned on her deathbed that she and her husband had adopted me and maybe my sister Louisa, but that's all I know.'

'So Louisa escaped, too,' Mr King said. For a moment he seemed lost in thought. Lizzie stood up and fetched more coffee and fresh oatcakes.

'Your finger!' Mr King suddenly shouted. 'Show me your hands.'

Lizzie put down the coffee pot and stretched out her hands for all to see. To her there was nothing wrong with them. They were clean, but not beautiful.

'Look,' Mr King said, pointing to her little fingers. He showed her his own. 'Mine too curve at the top. It's a family trait. I'm absolutely convinced you are Elizabeth's daughter. Is Louisa with you?'

'My sister died many years ago of cholera. She was much older than me and . . . '

'What? Did Martha survive as well? Please tell me she did.'

'I do vaguely remember, mainly in my dreams, that there were two older girls when I was little but I can't remember much about them.'

'I am confident I can prove you are my niece and I'd be delighted to welcome you back to the family. This is indeed a cause for celebration.'

*　*　*

It was Sunday morning. Susanna and Lizzie had decided, now that they were accepted back in Jacob's Creek, that they would attend the chapel and give thanks for their good health. Connor sat at the back of the chapel and afterwards followed them outside into the sunshine.

'Connor,' Lizzie called once they were back out in the street after the service.

'Miss Holden?'

Lizzie looked up at him, a little surprised. Hadn't he got into the habit of calling her Lizzie? Maybe that was only in her dreams.

'May I have a word with you?' she asked.

'Don't worry, I have the money for your jewellery safe and sound. I'll drop it by later. It's all there. I promise.'

'I never doubted it,' Lizzie told him. 'I wouldn't have given you my chains if I hadn't trusted you in the first place.'

'I suppose not.'

They fell into step as they walked back into the main part of the town. Susanna trailed behind. She and Thomas the pedlar were deep in conversation.

'Mrs Newham and I can never thank you enough for letting us use the cabin, but we are both in good health and assume you will need it back.'

Connor smiled.

'I have found other accommodation for the time being. There's no rush, but I dare say the King family will want you with them now.'

'But I don't know them and I couldn't leave Susanna. She's like a mother to me.'

'Don't be too hasty,' Connor warned her. 'It's better to have friends than enemies.'

'Wise words,' Thomas the pedlar

agreed as he strode up beside them.

They said their farewells. Susanna and Lizzie headed for their home, leaving Connor and Thomas outside the general store. The two women walked home in companionable silence, both deep in their own thoughts. Lizzie had no idea what it was that was on Susanna's mind but she had lots to contemplate.

She thought back to her conversation with Connor. Of course she did not want to make an enemy of Mr King and his family but neither did she feel she would fit into his home. She was used to doing things her own way and had enjoyed her independence since Mr and Mrs Holden had gone.

Even when she'd met Jeremiah and his mother, Lizzie had been keen to keep her own identity and she knew Susanna respected that. The woman had always been supportive and never tried to change her, not even her tomboyish ways.

A carriage passed them, sending up

clouds of dust from the dry road. Not many people owned a carriage. Lizzie glanced up, shielding her eyes from the fog of dust. It belonged to the Hamiltons.

Elijah was driving the horses while May and her father-in-law, Duke, were sitting in the back. They, too, had been in church.

In light of what she had now learned about her true identity she wondered if she should feel anger or even hatred toward the Hamilton males. Should she seek revenge? Should she at least try to uncover the truth?

As Lizzie walked along the now familiar route to what had become their home, she realised she felt no malice in her heart at all. She was angry with Elijah because she suspected he wasn't always kind and gentle to May but it was true that May had made up her mind to stay loyal to him and put up with his moods.

May was always the person to stand

up for her husband, saying that he could be a loving man. Then there was Duke Hamilton himself. Again she had no hard evidence that he had been responsible for any wrong-doing. He himself had been broken-hearted by Elizabeth's rejection. Perhaps she should actually feel sorry for him? Then there was Elijah, too, who had fallen for the daughter, Martha.

As Lizzie walked and saw the wooden cabin in the distance she recalled the preacher's words. His sermon had been about forgiveness. Lizzie decided that if May had found it in her heart to forgive Elijah and Duke Hamilton for what they may or may not have done, then she could too, but Lizzie wished she could make Elijah a more loving husband.

★ ★ ★

In due course, Connor arrived with the money he'd made from Mr King on Lizzie's behalf. He also handed her back the jewellery saying Mr King wanted her to keep it as it was meant to belong to her.

'This will see you right for a time,' he told them as he counted out the money for them all to see. 'I got a good price. I was expecting to have to barter but he paid up then and there.'

'So, now we have got enough to move on,' Lizzie said, looking firstly at Susanna and then at Connor.

'You've made it quite homely here,' he told them. 'I'm in no rush to be back, although I dare say there will come a time when I am no longer welcome where I'm living now.'

Lizzie wondered where he was now and if there was someone special in Connor's life. He struck her as being rather a loner. Elijah always had his men around him and Duke was never alone but Connor walked tall by himself.

Before he left, Connor did a tour of his cabin and grounds. He smiled at the little garden Lizzie had cultivated and was pleased to see the goats were well cared for.

'You have made yourself at home here.' He laughed. 'I think you should stay, at least for the time being.' Lizzie looked towards Susanna who nodded. She knew the older woman didn't want to move on again.

'In that case we'll stay put.'

'I'll put a fence around the place,' Connor offered. 'It'll help protect your crops and make it look a bit more like a homestead.'

'Thank you,' both Lizzie and Susanna said together, 'most kind.'

No sooner had Connor left when Thomas called by yet again. Lizzie had been surprised how much time he was spending in the area. She'd been led to believe he spent all his time travelling around selling his wares but, other than venturing out to the surrounding towns and villages, he always appeared to be drawn back here.

Lizzie filled a jug of ale and handed it to Susanna. She noticed the way

Thomas was looking at the older woman. Lizzie realised he wasn't here for the ale.

'I'll go and check on the goats,' she said, leaving them to carry on their conversation in private.

'Before you go,' Thomas said, 'I have a message from Mr King. He's seen his lawyer. Between them they've been keeping an eye on High Point but if you can prove to the lawyer that you are who he says you are, then the deeds will be transferred over. Not that there's much standing up there now, only a few stables and outbuildings . . . '

'But a fabulous view,' Lizzie finished his sentence. 'I had a good feeling when I was up there. I didn't understand it at the time. I thought I would feel overwhelmingly sad but instead I felt I was at peace there. I think I understand why now.'

'You're to go and see the lawyer,' Thomas continued.

'But how will I prove my identity? I have no papers to show who I am.'

'Just turn up. Like the rest of us, he will take one look at you and see whose daughter you are. Then, of course, you can tell him about how you and your sister were adopted and show him your hands and the undeniable family likeness. No more will need to be said.'

Lizzie didn't like the thought of going to see the lawyer. He was, by all accounts, a fierce man. People feared him more than the sheriff and the sheriff was a terrifying man she'd only seen twice — the first time when they first arrived in Jacob's Creek having been attacked on the outskirts of town and then when gangsters had tried to rob the bank.

However, once the lawyer saw her, she didn't need to introduce herself or explain why she was there. The man nodded and signed some papers, giving her a copy of the deeds for the land at High Point.

'What do I do now?' Lizzie asked the lawyer.

'Have you visited High Point?' he

asked. She nodded. 'In that case I would pay Mr King a visit. He is keen to celebrate your homecoming.'

'What if I don't want to come home to him?'

'As far as he's concerned, you're a miracle, you're back from the dead. He always felt something like this would happen but no-one believed him. Everyone thought he was just unable to accept what had really happened. I am glad he has been proven right.'

'I don't even know where he lives,' Lizzie explained. The lawyer gave her directions and she made that her next stop.

Time to Celebrate

Mr King was so thrilled to welcome Lizzie back to Jacob's Creek that he decided to throw a party in her honour. There was often little to celebrate in the quiet town where it was more common to mourn the dead than to open your arms to someone you thought you'd lost.

Mr King's barn was swept out. Bales of hay formed a raised stage at one end and were placed around the sides to be used as seating. A couple of fiddle players were booked and a bar set up.

'All you need now is your Sunday best,' Mr King told all his guests.

Lizzie grinned at Susanna when he took them aside. He had obviously seen their 'Sunday best' at church and not thought it up to much. Therefore he had insisted he buy them material and all the necessary trimmings in order to make themselves a new gown each.

All they had to do was to put it on his account and he would settle up at the end of the month. He'd already spoke with Samuel and Mary Franklin.

Susanna was beside herself with excitement. She'd had her eye on various fabrics already and just needed the excuse and the money to get her over to the general store hammering on their door for service.

Lizzie wasn't so enthusiastic. She owned two dresses, and that was sufficient in her book. One was her daily work dress which she could wear with or without her apron and then there was her best dress for special occasions — which were few and far between — so it had remained neatly folded in her chest since the day they had arrived, other than the time they went to give thanks at church.

'You'll never have the time to make two dresses,' Lizzie told Susanna. 'I suggest you concentrate on your own and either I'll ask May to make me one or borrow one of hers. We're about the same size and I've always liked the pale blue dress she wears.'

'You can't wear that!' Susanna cried out in horror.

'Why ever not? I think it's rather becoming.'

'For one thing it's her day dress and not special enough for the 'guest of honour' and secondly, she's been invited, and so no doubt she'll be busy making her own gown.'

'I still think you should make your own dress first and then, only if you have time, make a very simple one for me. I mean it. I don't want any frills or fancy bits.'

'I think I know you well enough now to know what you will like. In fact I've already had my eye on the perfect fabric. I hope she hasn't sold it already.'

'I doubt if there is much market for fancy dresses in this place,' Lizzie told her. 'I shouldn't worry.'

'But everyone is coming to this party.

We'll have to be quick and make our choices.'

'Surely not everyone.' Lizzie laughed. 'I thought it was just friends and family.'

'Mr King has a lot of friends,' Susanna told her. 'Now, don't make a face or be a spoilsport. It's rare for the town to have such good news and it's good that everyone is keen to celebrate. You've brought happiness to the place just by being here, don't you forget that.'

'I try to forget Duke and Elijah Hamilton driving us out of town when you were ill and if Connor hadn't spoken with them they wouldn't have allowed us an extra week.'

'And that's all in the past and to be forgotten. Things are different now and we must move on.'

'I'm happy for you to go and get the material and everything.'

'Maybe you would be, but I want you to show an interest and come along too. It'll be good for you to be seen about town.'

'But they all stare at me and I don't like it. It makes me feel like a freak.'

'You're a pretty lass, that's all. Believe me, one day you'll look back and wish someone would give you a second glance.'

'Like Thomas does with you?'

'What do you mean?' Susanna asked, her cheeks burning crimson like the logs in the fire.

'All I'm saying is that I've noticed how often he calls by to speak with you and how he gazes into your eyes, and . . . ' Lizzie grinned. 'I think you like him, too.'

'Thomas is a good man but I couldn't live his sort of life. I've really enjoyed being settled in one place. It wouldn't suit me, all that travelling around.'

★ ★ ★

Susanna had neglected her other chores but had managed to make herself and

175

Lizzie a dress each for the dance hosted by Mr King.

Thomas spent the afternoon cleaning out his little wagon and making it worthy of carrying Susanna and Lizzie to the barn. It was a warm and starry evening and there was enough food to feed the whole village.

Lizzie was surprised at how many people were there and how many of them she recognised. For the first time she felt she really belonged and decided she would ask Connor to take her back to High Point so she could see if it would be possible for her to build a little farmhouse where she and Susanna could live.

Lizzie caught a glimpse of Susanna, who was dancing with Thomas. In fact, he hadn't left her side since they arrived. Perhaps she wouldn't want to share her home with Lizzie after all?

Her thoughts returned to Connor. They hadn't seen so much of him recently as he no longer needed to drop off their groceries because they could freely come and go in the town once more.

Both she and Susanna had admitted how much they missed Connor's visits. He had always brought them news and entertained them with his stories.

And there he was standing, as handsome as ever, framed in the side door to the barn. He was looking around until he noticed Lizzie and smiled back at her.

To her surprise and delight he marched straight over to her and bent to kiss her hand as if she were as important as the sheriff's wife.

'Will you dance with me later?' he asked.

'Me? Dance?' Lizzie was horrified. 'I've never danced in my life. I don't know what to do.'

'Don't worry. The caller will guide us all. We just have to follow his instructions. Watch them now. You'll soon pick it up.'

Lizzie turned her head and watched Susanna and Thomas skipping around on the dance floor laughing away together. It looked as though they were having a good time and so was everyone else.

'I'm glad I've seen you,' Lizzie said.

Connor looked at her with his friendly smile.

'Are you?'

'I wanted to ask if you'd take me up to High Point sometime and let me have a look around? That's if it's no trouble?'

'No problem at all. I've been keeping it in good order for you. I hope you approve of what I've done.'

'I didn't realise you'd been up there.'

'I've been living in the stables since I vacated the cabin.'

Lizzie was shocked.

'Oh, no, I had no idea we turned you out of your home. You should never have offered it. I'm so sorry . . . I didn't know. How foolish of me not to realise.'

'The stables are not so bad.' Connor laughed. 'And once I knew High Point was yours, it seemed right that I should guard the place for you.

'When we go up there you can see I've made a start at clearing the old rubble away and cleaning up the outhouses. There's still a lot of work to do.'

'Thank you. I can't wait to see what you've done. I don't remember too much about the remains of the house. All I can think of is that wonderful view. I trust you haven't blocked that out.'

'The view is safe,' he told her. 'Now, how about we have a dance and then I can assure you you'll need some refreshments. It's thirsty work.'

As they walked towards the dance floor Lizzie noticed May in her new dress, a darker blue one this time with lace cuffs and collar. She smiled at Lizzie before Elijah pulled her away to the other side of the room.

Automatically Lizzie looked around for Duke Hamilton but there was no sign of him. Perhaps he was drinking at the bar? Maybe he hadn't been invited?

Connor took her hand and led her to the makeshift dance floor. The caller was asking for pairs to stand in groups of eight. Connor didn't let go of Lizzie's hand and she rather liked the feel of it.

Firstly they walked through the steps of the dance. Lizzie was given confidence by this but then the music started up and things got a lot faster.

She shouldn't have worried. Connor was always by her side to guide her through each step of the way and soon she got the hang of the steps and knew what to anticipate next.

'Was it so bad?' he asked as they bowed to each other at the end.

'You were right, it is thirsty work. Let's get a drink before the next dance.' Connor remained her partner all night long. Lizzie was perfectly happy with that and even on the dances where they had to swap partners, she could always look up and see Connor watching her as though he only had eyes for her. The one exception Connor made was to allow Mr King to have one dance with her.

'Thank you so much for putting this on. Everyone looks so happy.'

'They do, don't they?' Mr King agreed. 'I hadn't realised what a miserable lot we usually are. Don't tell anyone yet but I am thinking about making this an annual event. Other towns do this sort of thing, so why not Jacob's Creek?'

Lizzie hadn't really been looking forward to the evening but had put on a brave face for Susanna and for Mr King.

She had been pleasantly surprised by the dress Susanna had made for her. She had chosen a mustard-yellow gingham with matching ribbons in her hair. Her own dress had a gathered skirt that wasn't too full but showed off her trim figure while being easy to move in. Lizzie had not wanted a hoop under her skirt as some ladies wore.

Susanna's dress was a little more elaborate with lace at the cuffs and a little lace collar. Lizzie looked at her again and thought she looked years younger these days.

Lizzie wondered if perhaps she'd been making herself ill for years with the worry of her husband's drinking and then losing her only son. Now all her worries were in the past and Thomas the pedlar was showing her some genuine attention.

'You look deep in thought,' Connor whispered in her ear. The music was loud and it was hot inside the barn. 'Shall we step outside for some fresh air?'

'What do you think of my dress?' Lizzie asked Connor as she did a little twirl for him. 'Susanna made it for me. Isn't she clever?'

'I think you look beautiful, but then I thought you looked just as good when you got off that wagon with the gun still smoking in your hands. Do you remember the day you arrived at Jacob's Creek?'

'I sure do recall that day. I did think

this was the worst place ever, but now I'm not so sure.'

'For someone who felt like that you've hung around a long time.'

'Well, most of it was spent inside caring either for Jeremiah or for Susanna, but I'm not complaining. It's given me time to think about what is good in the world.'

'And what is good?' Connor asked with a smile. 'Was that kiss good?'

'What kiss would that be?' Lizzie asked pretending to be all innocent as if she could ever forget that kiss.

'Let me remind you.' Connor slipped his hands around her little waist and pulled her close to him. Gently he pressed his lips against hers as they melted together under the moonlight.

Lizzie reached up to stroke Connor's face. When she had first kissed his cheek she recalled how scratchy it had been. Today obviously he'd visited the barber and his face was surprisingly smooth.

All too soon they were joined by other people in need of the cooler, fresher air.

'Another dance?' Connor offered her his hand. Without a second thought she took it and was led on to the dance floor just in time for the last dance of the evening.

As they held each other by the hand Lizzie was more aware of Connor by her side than she had ever been before. He was a tall man with broad shoulders and yet he had proved himself to be nimble on his feet and gentle with his hands.

Skilfully he guided her into a turn and back as they promenaded around the barn. Lizzie liked to promenade with Connor lightly draping his arm around her shoulders whilst holding both her hands.

All too soon the evening drew to a close and Thomas helped Susanna and Lizzie into his cart ready for the homeward journey. Lizzie had thanked Mr King once again. She'd looked for

Connor to say goodnight but he had disappeared.

★   ★   ★

That night as Lizzie lay in bed, she thought about the evening that she had not been looking forward to. It had turned out to be so much better than she had feared.

For a start, Mr King had not singled her out and made some embarrassing speech. All he'd done was throw a party in her honour but not made a big thing about it. It was as if he had understood and she was grateful for that. Perhaps he was more family than she had given him credit for. In time, perhaps she'd get to know him better. The night had taught Lizzie a valuable lesson. In future she would be more willing to give new things a try and she would make more of an effort to get to know the townsfolk, many of whom had greeted her tonight.

As Lizzie was drifting off to sleep she

relived the wonderful moment of being in Connor's arms as he kissed her. His lips were so warm and soft. She could sense the hunger in them and yet he remained gentle as though not wanting to hurt her or to push her too far.

She touched her lip and imagined she could still feel Connor close beside her. With those thoughts she slipped into a deep sleeping and woke looking forward to seeing Connor again soon when he was to show her around High Point with a view to it perhaps becoming her new home.

Surprises

As it turned out, it was a few days before Connor was able to take Lizzie up to High Point. Her memory was of a burned out shack and the smell of smoke still in the air.

The view was just as beautiful as she recalled but now the charred wood had all but gone. The outbuildings had been repaired as well as the stables. Only the stone foundations were left of the original farmhouse. Connor was pointing to them.

'You could use them as your guide and rebuild, or I can move them away and start again. It's up to you.'

'Part of me would like to honour my family by keeping it the same, but then the other part of me would like a fresh start, a new chapter. What do you think?'

'It's not for me to say, but I agree

that perhaps it would be better to forget the old and start with something new that is yours.'

'I am going to ask Mr King if he would mind if I changed the name from High Point to something new like 'Journey's End' or 'Goat Corner'.'

'You're still keen to keep a goat herd, then?'

'It's what I know, and they would love it up here. I think Bill and Annie are going to need some more room soon anyway.'

'Bill and Annie?' Connor asked, looking confused.

'The goats you gave us. Susanna and I have called them after my parents, Bill and Annie Holden. And I think Annie must be due fairly soon.'

Connor and Lizzie spent the next hour discussing various plans for the land. For each suggestion Connor estimated how much it would cost her in building materials. He offered to do much of the building himself, perhaps with Thomas's help, in return for remaining on site where he'd made his own dwelling for the time being.

Lizzie returned to the little cabin that had become her home with lots to think about. She was hoping to be able to discuss her thoughts and ideas with Susanna but she was nowhere to be found.

Instead Lizzie went out to check on the goats. Annie looked a strange sight with the kid kicking away inside her as she waddled along grazing the grass and nibbling at the scraps Lizzie offered her.

Bill looked up as Lizzie approached. She sat on the veranda watching the goats. Bill had become quite protective of Annie lately and would rear up if anyone came into the garden.

She thought back to the land at High Point. She'd been so excited when she'd initially seen how Connor had already tidied up the place and made it look less like the remains of a gigantic bonfire. But whilst they were making plans she'd felt something wasn't right.

Now she looked at the little wooden cabin and realised what she'd been thinking was basically to pick it up and transport it up the hill and deposit it at High Point but now she realised that was not going to work.

Eventually Susanna came home looking very pleased with herself. Lizzie wondered if she'd met up with Thomas but it transpired she had been to the bank.

'And you'll never guess — we had more put away than I recalled.'

Lizzie remembered being sent to the bank when Jeremiah was first taken badly. Susanna had wanted the money put out of sight so that he couldn't be tempted to spend it and it had turned out to be a wise decision.

The extra money must be the reward she'd received for her part in capturing the gangsters who had tried to steal the money. She was only thankful their money had been kept safe.

'Does this mean you and Thomas might have a future together?'

'Good Lord, no, the money is yours.'

'Mine? How do you work that out?' Lizzie asked in surprise.

'It's what is left from the sale of your home, your farm where the Holdens brought you up. The money you gave to Jeremiah for your future. Unfortunately he'd spent some of it, but thankfully there is still a tidy sum.'

It was as if the sun had come out and lit up Lizzie's mind. Suddenly she could clearly see what it was she needed to do at High Point. She felt much happier now she knew where she had been going wrong.

Lizzie felt lighthearted all evening and insisted on helping Susanna with the tea which had become her role in their little household. They were just sitting down to their food when they heard the most peculiar noise outside. It was like an unearthly scream.

'Oh, no, that's Annie. She must have gone into labour.'

* * *

'Well, aren't we well and truly blessed?' Susanna declared as she and Lizzie viewed the two kids that had been born that evening. Bill was standing protectively over his family while Annie was licking her kids clean.

'Two milkers, too, that's good news,' Lizzie said. 'This has been the most perfect day.' With that, she threw her arms around Susanna and gave her a hug.

'I have so much to tell you about my time at High Point with Connor. I'm keen to know what you think.'

'And are you going to move up there to live?'

'Connor says we can stay here for as long as we want. It's going to take some time to fix up the place on the hill but that's where I'd eventually want to be. I think you'll be happy there, too.'

'I wouldn't want to be any trouble,' Susanna, looking down in her lap. 'I guess you'll want to help Connor actually build the homestead?'

'I'll do what I can, but I think he's

going to enrol the help of Thomas, unless he's away travelling, of course.'

'And for my part,' Susanna told her, 'I can keep you all fed.'

'That's settled, then. I'll speak to Mr King first and then to Connor. I've got an idea of what would work up there.'

As luck would have it, the very next day Lizzie saw Mr King in Jacob's Creek.

She thanked him again for the dance and told him once more how much she had enjoyed it and how she was already looking forward to the next one.

He had announced at the end of the evening that he would host the dance as an annual event and everyone had cheered.

Lizzie went through her ideas for High Point suggesting that she put a new building of a different shape on the site of the old one. That way she could honour her family while still looking forward to happier times.

'That's a grand idea,' he told her with a smile.

'Just one more thing,' Lizzie asked as she took a deep breath. 'Would you be very upset if I changed the name from High Point to Goat Corner?'

'It's probably time we moved on but folk round here will go on calling it High Point for many years to come. Call it what you want with my blessing, but don't expect the rest of the townsfolk to change the habits of a lifetime.' He chuckled.

'I have some more news, too.' Lizzie was bursting with excitement. 'Connor gave me two goats a while back. They have just produced two females.

'Susanna and I would like to call them Martha and Louisa after my sisters. You'll have to come and meet them sometime.'

'You'll need some sturdy fencing if you've got goats,' he warned her, 'but Connor will advise you well. He's a good man, quiet, but hard working and honest, which is a lot more than you can say about many of the men around here.'

Lizzie blushed at the way Mr King was looking at her. She knew he must have noticed she'd danced every dance with Connor Riordan. Maybe he'd even been aware of their kiss. Jacob's Creek was not a place to hold a secret for long.

They bade their farewells and carried on with their own business. Lizzie was pleased to find she and Susanna were now being treated more like locals than as visitors.

Even on her journey from the cabin to the main street this morning a couple of people had nodded and said, 'Howdy.'

As Lizzie went about her chores she realised she liked the feeling of belonging that she now felt. Was this what made somewhere home, she wondered. She was aware too that her loyal companion Susanna felt the same and already Susanna was making a name for herself with her neat stitching and skilled dressmaking.

The New Homestead

Connor, with Lizzie as his assistant, did much to transform the land that had once been known as High Point. However, they could not have completed the new homestead so quickly had it not been for the help of so many of the villagers.

Hardly a day went past when no-one came to see what they were up to. Someone would ride by and stay to help for an hour or two, then someone else would bring timber or tools to make the job quicker.

Connor was true to his word and had worked tirelessly to make Lizzie's dreams become reality. He had raised an eyebrow at her design but when she told him to trust her, he had gone along with her wishes.

Lizzie could not fault Connor in any way, other than the fact that since the night of the dance he had seemed reserved and cool towards her.

On one occasion she had tried to flirt a little with him but Connor had not responded. Lizzie had spoken to Susanna about it and was told to give him time.

That was all very well, Lizzie thought, but Connor was a handsome man and she was all too aware that she was not the only single, unattached female in the area.

Lizzie had expected it to take many months to take shape but in no time at all a new home stood proudly on the top of the hill. It wasn't totally finished but the main structure was up.

The whole area was well fenced in. The goats had a big field with shelter in one corner and rocks for them to climb upon and view the world as they liked to do.

Late one afternoon Duke Hamilton drove his daughter-in-law May over to see how the building work was coming along.

'It's very good of you to call,' Lizzie told them. She greeted May with a warm hug and introduced her to the new goats. She nodded to Duke who went to speak with Connor.

'Thank you so much for coming to see what we're doing here,' Lizzie told her friend. 'I hope when it's finished you'll be a regular visitor. We will be close neighbours, after all.'

'It was actually Duke's suggestion that we drive over.'

'Really? I am surprised.'

'Elijah has been away a lot lately. In the evenings the men all sleep in their quarters near the stables. It is only Duke and me in the main house and we've talked a lot more lately. He's mellowed a great deal. I sometimes wonder if Elijah will grow up to be more like him.'

'That's good news,' Lizzie said, 'but it's Elijah you need to be talking to.'

'I will try when he returns. They're moving buffalo up to the plains. It'll take them several days, if not weeks, but he enjoys riding out with his men. Sometimes I think he wishes he hadn't married me.'

'Surely not! Why ever do you think that?'

'He hardly shows me any attention,' May said but she didn't cry. 'I am being too harsh on the man. He buys me gifts. It's just that that night at the dance I saw you and Connor so happy together, and it made me think that he still loves another.'

'And what does Duke say about this?'

'He tells me I've nothing to worry about. It's just Elijah's way. In fact he did remind me what he was like when I went away for a few days and he was worried that I wouldn't come back.'

'Well, there you are then.'

'I will try and look my best for him when he comes home, though.'

'Have you missed him?' Lizzie asked.

'Elijah is like two different people depending on whether is leg is giving him pain or not.'

'Can't the doctor give him something?'

'If only it were that easy,' May said. 'It's something we all have to live with.'

While Lizzie and May had been talking, it seemed Duke had offered Connor several of his men to help with the roof of the house and extending the stables.

'With their help we'll have it done in no time at all,' Connor told her, 'but we'll need a lot of stew in the pot. They're hungry men.'

Although Lizzie and Susanna now spent most of their days working away at Goat Corner, they fed the goats and returned home to the cabin each evening, leaving Connor to his solitary sleeping quarters in the stables with his horse.

Lizzie loaded their cart for the journey home one day after they had been busy working on the new house. The goats had now been driven up to the new dwelling and were enjoying the lush grass. Connor was petting Louisa, the smallest goat. She was jumping up at him playfully.

'He's a handsome man,' Susanna whispered.

'Yes, he is certainly a fine-looking man,' Lizzie replied, 'but don't give me that look. He is only a friend.'

'And I suppose if you were to marry him, I would have to stay at the cabin on my own.'

'No, that would never do — and besides, I'm not marrying Connor.'

Neither of the women had noticed that Connor had finished playing with the goat and had wandered over toward them in order to bid them goodnight.

'The only reason she isn't marrying me,' Connor said with a smile, 'is because I haven't asked her yet. But, Mrs Newham, when I do ask her, and if she accepts, then you are very welcome to live with us here.'

Lizzie and Susanna both turned to face Connor with their mouths wide open.

Connor sank down to his knees.

'Miss Lizzie Holden, will you do me the great honour of becoming my wife?'

'I would . . . ' Lizzie began. 'But you've been ignoring me and avoiding me since the dance.'

'I've been busy building your house!'

'You could at least smile at me once in a while or maybe even look pleased to see me.'

'There are many men in the town who would be a better catch for you,' Connor told her, standing with his hat in his hands. 'Perhaps you would prefer one of them?'

'No, Connor,' Lizzie told him as she looked up into his handsome face. 'I only have eyes for you but I shall want you to be happier to see me if we are to be wed.'

'I think I can manage that.' Connor laughed. 'Is that a yes?'

'Lizzie Riordan, I think I like the sound of that,' Lizzie said playfully. 'Yes, Connor, I would love to be your wife.'

Susanna threw up her arms in delight

and hugged them both.

'And what Connor said is true, you are most welcome to live with us here — in fact, I insist,' Lizzie said.

'Let me finish loading the cart,' Susanna said, as she wiped away a few happy tears. 'You two will have things to talk about, no doubt.'

Connor took Lizzie's hand and led her to the back of the homestead, the part where they could stand on the new veranda, smelling the freshly sawn timber and gaze out at the barren but beautiful landscape in front of them.

'One day,' Connor said, 'I would like to sit here of an evening with you on our veranda and watch our children playing in the yard or running after the goats. Would you like that too?'

'Oh, Connor, there is so much to take in.' Lizzie laughed. 'I can think of nothing I would love more than to spend my evenings with you and perhaps in time we will have a family of our own. I will do my very best to be a good wife to you.'

'And I a good husband to you,' Connor said, pulling her into his arms and holding her close. Lizzie could feel him next to her. She was aware of his heartbeat pounding away as he held her.

She could feel his gentle kisses as his lips caressed the top of her hair.

'Come here,' he said, 'I want to kiss you and then I suppose I'll have to let you go but tonight I shall dream of you.'

'Don't you dream of me every night?' Lizzie teased. 'I think of you.'

'Do you?'

'Of course! I often dream of you and the goats . . . but mainly of you.'

Connor laughed with her and then lightly pulled her back into his arms. His lips found hers and they sealed their engagement with a kiss.

Wedding Plans

Lizzie had no idea how much the plans for her wedding would take her away from the work on the new home. The shell of the building had been finished for some time but the interior needed to be transformed from an empty barn into an inviting home.

'But we have to get the homestead finished,' she told Susanna. 'Otherwise we'll have nowhere to live, and don't say we've got the cabin because you know it will be so much easier once we've moved everything up here.'

'I'm just saying,' Susanna repeated, that we need to get you measured up for a dress or you'll be walking down the aisle in that tatty day dress.'

'And would that be so bad?' Lizzie asked. 'I don't really care what I wear, it's who I'm marrying.'

'And Connor is a good choice but I

bet May will make sure he's looking dapper in his suit. It's the least you can do to look like a bride.'

'I'll come into town with you tomorrow,' Lizzie agreed.

'But you said that yesterday, and the day before.'

'And I've told you to concentrate on making something for yourself. You know I'll be happy in anything.' Lizzie smiled.

'It's traditional for a bride to wear white,' Susanna told her.

She was getting quite short with Lizzie, even though she knew she was only trying to work hard to get their homestead ready before the wedding day.

On occasions May would visit from the Hamilton ranch and together she would sit and sew with Susanna while Lizzie would be in the yard with Connor putting the finishing touches to the stables or making extra housing for the goats.

Thomas the pedlar was a regular

visitor. He often helped them with the building work.

'Good day, Thomas,' Lizzie said one morning when the pedlar had appeared at their door. He took off his hat and ran his fingers through his hair. Lizzie thought he looked a bit uncomfortable but could not think why.

'Is there something wrong?' she asked him.

'I'd like a word, miss, in private like.'

'Of course,' Lizzie said. She suspected Susanna had been complaining to him about her avoidance of going into the town to choose wedding dress material.

'What is it you want to say?'

Again he fidgeted from foot to foot.

'This wedding,' he began. 'I was thinking. You having no family and all . . . Do you want me to give you away? You know, to walk you down the aisle?'

'Oh,' Lizzie said taken aback by his surprise offer. It was the last thing she had been expecting him to say. She was mighty touched by his offer.

'Unless of course Mr King is doing the honours?'

'Mr King has given us his blessing,' Lizzie told the pedlar, 'but he's not a well man at the moment. I wouldn't want to trouble him with anything and he might feel it was his duty.

'I hadn't given it any thought but now you mention it, I would be delighted if you would escort me to the church and walk me down the aisle.'

★　★　★

As the wedding day grew closer they moved the majority of their things from the cabin to the new homestead. The way Lizzie had designed it, there were sleeping quarters at each end with a communal living space in the centre with a large kitchen and fireplace.

Susanna was to sleep at one end of the house while she and Connor would have a room at the other end, near the stables.

Susanna took the parcel she'd given

Lizzie when she'd told her to leave town. It was still all wrapped up, as it had been intended as her wedding gift to Lizzie. It was a beautifully embroidered nightdress.

Carefully she unwrapped the soft gown and set it on the pillow in what would become Lizzie's new bedroom.

Meanwhile, Lizzie took the cart and drove into town. Her first trip was to see Mrs Franklin at the general store.

'Mrs Franklin,' Lizzie began, putting her list to one side. 'I've been meaning to ask you — were you the kind person who often left us bread when we were holed up at Connor's cabin?'

'Firstly, you really must call me Mary and yes, occasionally I did leave the odd loaf or bacon. It was the least I could do. But Rachel Bradley from the hotel and Miss Harper also left you things.'

'Miss Harper?'

'She's the school mistress. She's taught practically everyone in town. I've seen her heading down your way with a basket of berries or mushrooms.'

'But I don't even know her.'

'But she knew of you and she has a kind heart. I know none of us wanted to catch Jeremiah's fever and we were all worried when Susanna fell ill, but I think that was just exhaustion from looking after him and grieving when he went.

'I know we must have come across as unfriendly at that time, but we did our bit.'

'Well, Susanna and I are grateful, very grateful and in time we'll make sure we can pay you back in kind.'

'There's no need for that,' Mary Franklin told her. 'We all look out for each other in this town. I guess you'll have worked that out for yourself by now.'

'I sure have and that's why we're making it our town, too,' Lizzie told her. 'Now, I've come about . . . '

'The dress!' Mary interrupted. 'You're cutting it a bit fine, lass. Poor Mrs Newham is tearing her hair out over you having nothing to wear. I'm worried it will make her ill again.'

'But the homestead is finished and we'll have a roof over our heads. Surely that is more important than a dress?'

'Many would argue it wasn't.' Mrs Franklin laughed. 'Now come here. It so happens I have a dress that might fit you a treat. Come round the back and try it on.'

'But I only came in to order rope and hay for the goats.'

'It'll only take a few minutes of your time, and think how pleased and relieved Mrs Newham will be if you can tell her you've got a suitable white gown to wear.'

Reluctantly Lizzie agreed and followed Mrs Franklin into a little room at the back of the shop. Mary Franklin called out to her husband to mind the shop for a few minutes.

'There now, what do you think?'

Lizzie looked at herself in Mrs Franklin's mirror. She was dressed in a long white gown of a simple design.

'Stand up tall, girl.'

Lizzie did as she was told while Mrs Franklin scooped up her hair and tied it neatly with white ribbons.

Once she had finished, Lizzie turned from side to side, hardly recognising the reflection in the mirror.

Quite a different image stood in front of her. It was one of a woman about to become a wife. She hoped Connor would always be proud of his wife as she was of him.

She thought how much she had grown up and learned since arriving in Jacob's Creek engaged to another man.

She thought again of Connor. He was always the first person to volunteer to help someone. When she, Jeremiah and Mrs Newham had originally driven into town, their driver having been killed in an attack, it was Lizzie steering the horses and Connor was there to greet them and offer his assistance.

Since then, she realised, Connor and his loyal sister May had quietly offered their friendship and their help every step of the way. One day Lizzie would find a way to pay them back.

'What do you think?' Mrs Franklin asked. 'You're a bit skinny. I could take it in?'

'It's perfect just as it is,' Lizzie told her.

'So, what's up?' Mrs Franklin asked. 'I can see a troubled look in your eye.'

'It's lovely and I'm very grateful but I was wondering if it would hurt Susanna's feelings if I buy this dress rather than take up her offer to make me one? The last thing I want to do is to upset anyone, least of all Mrs Newham.'

'If you'd have asked me a month ago, I would have agreed with you, but you've run out of time and Mrs Newham would want to do a good job and make you the best dress ever. You're like a daughter to her, after all.'

'So, will she be happy if I take this one?'

'She has spoken with me on many occasions.' Mrs Franklin gave a smile and Lizzie knew the two women had become good friends.

'Believe me, she will be relieved. I know she'd have loved to have made your wedding dress but it hasn't worked out that way and she's accepted it. She's always got your happiness at heart.'

'In that case I'll have it — it's lovely,' Lizzie said and danced around. 'I never thought I'd feel so at home in a dress. Honestly I didn't.'

'So, shall I put some lace around the neck and the sleeves and perhaps a ribbon at the waist or . . . '

'No, no, no!' Lizzie laughed. 'Leave it just as it is. I love it.'

'Well . . . if you're sure,' Mrs Franklin said reluctantly. But none the less she slipped a dainty lace-edged handkerchief in with the dress as she carefully wrapped it up.

* * *

When Lizzie arrived back at Goat Corner she was not surprised to see the carriage from the Hamilton ranch. May often visited them and she could just picture Susanna and May putting the finishing touches to their dresses ready for the big day.

However, when she entered her new home she was surprised to find it was not May who had called on them, but Duke Hamilton himself.

'Connor's round the back,' Lizzie told him.

'It's you I've come to see.'

'Oh, no — is it May, is she ill?'

'No, May is fine and very much looking forward to your wedding. She is delighted you're marrying her brother and can't wait to officially have you as her sister.'

'I am looking forward to that, too,' Lizzie told him. 'So what is it you want from me?'

'May wondered if you had anyone to give you away,' Duke said. 'I know Mr King is unwell and that you have no kin. I am like a father to May, less so to Connor but he has my respect.'

'Thank you. That's such a kind, and unexpected offer ... ' Lizzie began. 'Unfortunately, Thomas the pedlar has already offered and I have accepted, but I look forward to seeing you at the wedding.'

'There is just one other thing.' Duke looked up and gazed for a moment into Lizzie's eyes. 'May tells me you intend to keep a herd of goats here — that you will be selling their milk and making cheese.'

'That's correct.'

'In that case, as a wedding gift, I would like to offer you some goats. Connor can come with me to market sometime and choose the ones he wants.' Duke hesitated a moment. 'Or you could come, if you'd like?' he added.

'I would like that very much. That's a very generous offer and most welcome. I shall make sure I send you and May a basket of produce once we're up and running.'

'In that case I'll bid you good day.'

'Good day, Mr Hamilton, thank you again. Connor and I will be delighted to see you at the wedding and to go to market with you soon.'

Once Duke Hamilton had gone Lizzie went into the back yard to tell Connor and Susanna the good news.

'I had to admit, when he first offered to give me away, I wondered if I could trust him. May had said he has mellowed and I have to agree he has been very generous.'

'There was never any firm evidence of any wrong doing,' Connor reminded her.

'And he's always been good to May. It can't have been easy for him being humiliated by Elizabeth King and then being blamed for her death.

'Then, when he did marry, later in life, his wife died in childbirth, so he and a series of housekeepers brought up Elijah. He's not had a happy life.'

The Big Day

On the day of the wedding Susanna was up early doing her chores and fussing around Lizzie.

'It's just as well I don't get married every day,' Lizzie laughed, 'we'd never get anything done.'

Once Lizzie had fed the goats and seen to the horses, collected the eggs and fed the chickens she returned to the house. Susanna had filled the tin bath for her and had hung up her dress with bunches of lavender to give it a pleasant smell.

'Come on, girl, you want to look your best, don't you?'

'Of course I do, but if I clean up too much Connor won't even recognise me.'

'Just get in that tub.' Susanna laughed. 'We'll wash your hair and I'll pin it up for you.'

Somehow Susanna managed to transform Lizzie from a working farm hand into a lady-like and elegant bride.

In amongst all the preparations, Thomas the pedlar arrived. Lizzie and Connor were getting married in the chapel opposite Goat Corner, the one where Lizzie's true parents had been married and she had been baptised, not that she remembered any of that.

It meant there was no need for a cart or wagon, Thomas was just going to escort her across the dusty road and into the chapel at the appointed time.

'Go on,' Lizzie said to Susanna as the time approached. 'Off you go, and we'll follow on in a moment.'

Susanna looked at Thomas dressed in his Sunday best.

'Whatever you do, don't let her go and pet those darn goats while she's all dressed up.'

'I'll keep an eye on her,' he promised.

Although Lizzie was nervously excited about her own special day, she did notice the look Susanna exchanged with Thomas. There was definitely an intimacy between them and they always treated each other with a tenderness Lizzie wanted to share with Connor.

'Have you ever thought of settling down?' Lizzie asked him once Susanna had made her way across the road to the chapel.

'Me? No. I've never found the right woman, although perhaps I have now.'

'There's room here for both you and Susanna and we'll need someone to take our goods to market on a regular basis.'

'I don't honestly know if I'd be able to settle,' he admitted. 'I've been on the road all my life.'

'You've been around here quite often these past few months.'

'That is true, and you have become like a family to me.' Thomas wiped away a tear.

'Speaking of which, now's the time to walk you over to Connor waiting in the church. We'd better not be too much longer or Susanna will think I've let you muck out the stables.'

Thomas stood up tall and Lizzie put her arm through his and together they left her new home, ready to start a new life with the man she loved.

They couldn't see anything because of the dust but they could certainly hear the loud thumping of hooves on the road. There were clouds of dust, swirling around like smoke making them cough as they hurried toward the chapel's entrance.

Someone had put flowers at the arched doorway. Lizzie smiled just as she was hit on the back of the head and everything went black.

★   ★   ★

It was Susanna who had slipped out from the coolness of the chapel to see what had become of the bride. She'd told Thomas in no uncertain words that he was to prevent her from doing any more chores that morning.

She was ready in her dress looking beautiful and all she had to do was walk straight across the road. So whatever could have happened to them?

Susanna almost tripped over Thomas as she left the chapel in a hurry.

'What's wrong? What are you doing lying down there? Where's Lizzie?'

Thomas sat up and rubbed his head. He had a dazed look about him.

'We heard horses, lots of them. We were just about to go in when someone hit me from behind and I don't remember any more. Where's Lizzie? Is she all right?'

Hearing the commotion, Connor and the rest of the congregation poured out into the churchyard to discover the bride had vanished into thin air.

Connor looked over at his sister. She'd gone a deathly white. She'd been sitting next to her father-in-law, Duke Hamilton. Her husband Elijah was still out of town. Or was he?

Connor and some of the other men

studied the hoof marks on the sandy soil.

'Looks like they went this way,' one said and immediately a posse were up on their horses in search of the missing bride.

Unfortunately, the trail came to a dead end when they reached the river and there was no easy way to pass. It was decided they would divide into four groups and continue their search north, south, east and west.

'They can't have got too far,' Connor told them. 'Please bring her back safely, that's all I ask.'

All day Connor and his closest friends searched the area to the west. They looked everywhere. There were no signs of fresh hoof-prints but there were some caves which Connor felt sure would make a good hiding place if one were needed.

There was no sign of his bride. Reluctantly as the sun began to set he had to give up his search for the evening. He and his men made their way back to Mr King's barn.

Mr King had very kindly offered, as his wedding gift, to host a dance again at his barn which was close to the chapel.

It had been agreed that the four groups would return to the barn — hopefully one of them with Lizzie, as soon as she'd been found.

Connor had been the last person back to the barn after his search had proved to be in vain. Now he could only hope that someone else had found her and that she was all right.

There was no such news. The men looked glum and shook their heads.

'We did find this, though.' One man, who had been searching in the north, held up a dusty, torn white gown. It was plain and simple with no lace. Both Mrs Franklin and Susanna gasped.

'Oh no, where did you find it?'

The men told them of the exact spot.

'We piled up stones so we'd find it again. Believe me, we searched every rock in the area. There was no sign of Lizzie.'

★ ★ ★

At first light Connor, who had hardly slept, set out again, this time in a northerly direction with the men who had found Lizzie's wedding dress.

'You must assume the worst,' one man told Connor.

'I know my Lizzie,' he told them. 'I bet she'd put up a fight and believe me the first chance she'd have she'd ditch the dress, but where can she be?'

Another day was spent searching. The whole town came out to look for her. No stone was left unturned.

Everyone played their part in the search. Thomas took a break from the hunting and returned to Goat Corner to feed the animals and check everything was as it should be.

Connor didn't return to the barn to sleep that night. He made himself a camp near where the dress had been found. He had a fitful night but managed a few hours of sleep only because he knew if he didn't get any rest he would be of no use the following day and he had to find Lizzie before it was too late.

She'd already been missing too long and the sun was baking hot and she had no water, no food and no shade as far as he knew.

He stirred early. Only a handful of men were now with him. It was decided they would return to the barn. They all had farms to run and work to do.

They returned with a heavy heart but praying there would be good news before the sun set, although deep in their hearts they feared the worst.

Duke, despite being an old man, had volunteered to stay with Connor. Duke made them coffee. Connor was sitting on his haunches as he drank the hot liquid and chewed on some bacon, knowing he needed to keep his own strength up.

As he glanced up, something caught his eye. He ran over to a cactus nearby.

'She went this way,' he called. Duke grabbed the coffee pot and kicked the fire to put it out and went to join Connor.

'Look, she's left me a trail. I knew she would.'

'Maybe she just caught her dress on the thorn. They're mighty prickly, those beasts.'

'No, don't you see? Her dress was left over there but it was already torn. Mrs Franklin showed me, the hem had been ripped off and this is too high for the hem to have been caught naturally. She must have wrapped it around here for a reason.'

Duke looked a little more closely at the cactus and nodded.

'I see what you mean but would the girl really have thought to do something like that?'

'She's not any old girl.' Connor laughed for the first time in days. 'She's my Lizzie, and she must have escaped from them or at least be leading us in their direction.'

Duke Hamilton didn't look so sure but he couldn't argue with the evidence and followed Connor in hunting for more scraps of the white material.

'Here's another,' Connor said after an hour. This time there were just a few strands of material caught on a large cylindrical cactus. It had thick white needles that could pierce a man's skin.

'These could have just blown here on the wind,' Duke warned. 'I don't want you to get your hopes up. She's been out here over two days.

'I don't suppose she's got water or shade and if she's still alive, which I doubt, she'll be in a bad way. With her colouring the sun will burn her skin and she'll die of thirst.'

'This is Lizzie Holden we're talking about. She's the most resourceful person I know. If anyone can survive out here it will be her.'

Duke Hamilton didn't look convinced but Connor was busy looking for the next clue.

They found it a short while later. There was more vegetation around the base of some hills. Connor had never travelled out this way before but Duke knew the area well as it was nearer his son's ranch and he often rode this way.

'There's some good shade in those hills but they're further away than you think. I doubt she'd have the strength to make it all the way over there, unless she was on a horse or they've still got her with them.'

'She wouldn't know that they're so far away. I bet that's where she's headed.' Connor was all the more determined and once Duke had seen the most recent piece of material, even he could tell it had been carefully tied in place.

It was clear to see it hadn't just been blown by the wind and caught on a cactus.

It gave him hope. He realised it

meant she was probably on her own otherwise she'd never have been given the chance to tie clues to prickly plants.

As much as Connor wanted to run and run in the direction of the hills he knew he had to stop himself and force himself to take it slowly while he continued to look for clues along the way.

'Is this another one?' Duke asked.

Sure enough, another bit of hem was flying like the American flag from the stem of yet another prickly cactus.

'By rights she should be cut to bits by now but there's no sign of blood.'

'I told you she's one resourceful woman.' 'Thanks for sticking by me,' Connor added and shook the man's hand. 'No hard feelings.'

'Come on,' Duke said, sounding more optimistic. 'I'm sure we're getting close.'

'Lizzie!' Connor called out her name a couple of times but it was lost on the breeze.

Just as sun was setting they reached

the base of the hills. Both men were exhausted. They were tired, hungry and thirsty but neither of them ready to stop their hunt.

'What's that?' Duke asked pointing to markings in the sandy soil. Connor bent to have a closer look. He examined the rest of the area.

'It looks fresh.'

With renewed vigour they continued to look. Just as they were about to set up camp for the night, Connor found Lizzie curled up in a ball in the shadow of two rocks. She was dressed in men's clothing.

'Lizzie?' he called gently, not wanting to frighten her. 'It's me, Connor, you're safe at last.'

Lizzie opened her eyes with a look of panic, took one glance at Connor and went back to sleep.

'I bet she thinks she's dreaming.' Duke shook his head. 'The poor girl's exhausted.'

Duke handed Connor a blanket which he draped over her. Duke had done a recce of the place and was confident they were alone. He nodded to Connor who was beginning to start a fire and brew up a welcome hot drink.

Lizzie woke to the smell of hot coffee and meat sizzling on a makeshift spit. She had never smelled anything so good or so welcome.

'Connor? Duke?' she said in surprise.

Connor opened his arms and hugged her as though he was never, ever going to let her out of his sight again.

Safe at Last

'So, Lizzie, do you know what happened?' Connor asked as the three of them sat around the fire.

'Thomas and I were at the church door. I was so pleased because someone had thought to leave flowers at the entrance and they looked so pretty and I was so happy I could have cried and then all of a sudden I felt something on the back of my head.' She reached up and winced.

Connor leaned over and gently felt the lump still on the back of her head.

'The next thing I knew I had been thrown over the back of a horse and taken away at speed. My mouth was so dry from the dust and I couldn't see because the grit got in my eyes and in my hair and I had this awful headache, but I'm not stupid.'

'No-one ever thought you were.'

'Even though I was being bounced around on the horse I was slowly coming to my senses and I could hear what was being said. When we finally stopped and they made camp I acted really sleepy and drowsy as though I'd had too much whisky or the doctor's medicine.'

'Good thinking.'

'They didn't take much notice of me. I think they thought it would be easier if I died and then they could have left me.'

'Do you know who they were?' Duke asked. 'Did you recognise anyone?'

'I didn't want to show too much interest because I didn't want them to think I was a threat. I did wonder if one of them was Reece from your ranch but I couldn't be sure. There was no-one I could definitely identify.'

'Reece?' Duke said thoughtfully. 'I thought he was rounding up buffalo with Elijah.'

Lizzie continued with her tale.

'The men had an argument. They

were all talking round the camp-fire. Some of them said they should just leave me there, others said they couldn't do that.'

'How many of them were there?' Connor asked her.

'Maybe half a dozen or so,' Lizzie told him. 'Perhaps there were more. I'm not really sure.'

'Did they say who'd put them up to it?'

'No.'

'Who was their leader?'

'I don't know. In fact none of them seemed to know what they were meant to do. It all sounded a bit disorganised, if you ask me.

'I got the impression they didn't really want to be there or involved in any kidnapping. Anyway they drank too much and slept deeply which suited me just fine. You wouldn't believe the sound of about six men snoring, it was enough to wake the dead.

'Anyway, I'd made my plan. One man was the look-out and he'd settled a little away from the main camp but he too was deeply asleep so, forgive me, but I took his clothes, his water bottle and his knife.'

Connor laughed at the thought.

'I bet he woke with a surprise and a bad head.'

'He's not the only one with a bad head,' Lizzie reminded them. 'I ran away from them and then when I thought it was safe I ditched the dress.

'Believe me, you can't run easily in a long dress. I kept tripping up and even though the man's clothes were too big for me, they were better. I tore the hem and left you a trail. Did you find it?'

'We certainly did and that's what led us to you.'

'I felt awful tearing the beautiful gown and wondered if Mrs Franklin would ever forgive me, but by then the dress was dusty and torn that I don't think she'd have recognised it anyway.'

'She'll just be pleased to have you back — as will the whole town.'

'Was I missed?' Lizzie asked in surprise.

'A bride doesn't go missing on the steps of the church and no-one take any notice.' Connor laughed, squeezing her hand. 'The whole town has been out searching the entire area. For all I know they're still searching now.'

'And Thomas?' Lizzie asked quietly. 'Is he all right? He was standing beside me. I hope he wasn't hurt.'

'He was knocked on the head but they only took you which makes me wonder why.'

'Is there someone who doesn't want you to be wed?' Duke asked, looking from one to another.

Both Lizzie and Connor shook their heads.

'I can't think of anyone.'

'Sadly, I can,' Duke said bitterly.

'Elijah?' Connor asked. 'But isn't he away chasing buffalo?'

'That's what May and I have been

told but he's been gone a mighty long time. She had hoped he'd be back for the wedding. We were so pleased to be invited. I mean, I would have understood if we were left off the guest list, under the circumstances.'

'But why would he do such a thing?' Lizzie asked. 'I mean, he may once have wanted to marry my sister Martha but by all accounts I don't look so much like her. I take after my mother.'

'You do,' Duke agreed. 'Your sisters took after your father but you are the spitting image of your mother.'

'So why would Elijah kidnap me and spoil my wedding? I've never done anything to upset him.'

'Neither have I,' Connor added. 'It doesn't make sense.'

'And surely now he's happily married to May and . . . '

'I know he's my one and only son and his mother, God rest her soul, would have doted on him, but he's a troubled boy who's grown into a troubled man.'

'So you think it was Elijah's doing?' Lizzie asked.

'No, I'm sure Elijah is far away from here and will have dozens of men to vouch for him, but if we ever catch any of the men who took you away, I bet they'll have been paid handsomely for their part in his plan. Not that we'll be able to trace the money back to Elijah but I can bet it was him who paid them.'

'Reece does work for him,' Lizzie said quietly. 'I can't be sure it was him but I would like to know if he's got an alibi for the last few days.'

'And you can be sure I'll be speaking to him as soon as we get you back home safely.'

'It doesn't really matter now,' Connor said. 'The main thing is that you're safe.'

'But she might have died,' Duke told him. 'I would want them hanged.'

'Let's leave that for the judge. For now we need to rest. It'll be a long journey home tomorrow but a great welcome when we get there.'

★ ★ ★

News of Lizzie's story, no doubt with several embellishments, began to spread and by the time Duke took Connor to market to choose some goats to add to the breeding stock at Goat Corner, even they had heard a version of Lizzie's tale.

Susanna was worried about Lizzie. She felt she wasn't quite the same as she used to be. Susanna fussed round her like a mother hen.

'I'm all right, at least I will be,' Lizzie kept telling her but she was glad Susanna never left her side and Thomas had taken to sleeping on the veranda as a self-imposed personal sheriff.

Duke and May decided not to say anything immediately to Reece but to keep their ears open for mutterings amongst their men.

It wasn't long before Duke overheard

two men teasing Moses for having a woman strip him of his clothes when he was supposed to have been the look-out. The time had come for the Duke to travel into town and seek out the sheriff.

Reece and Moses were hauled in but neither of them would name any of their fellow kidnappers, although they did admit to being party to the crime. They swore they were only carrying out orders and didn't wish her any harm.

Another date was set for the wedding. This time Lizzie had asked if she and Connor could just have a very quiet service at the end of Sunday morning prayers but Susanna persuaded her that the whole village had been out looking for her and she owed them the chance to celebrate with her and Connor.

Lizzie knew from all the kind words she'd received, that this had been true and she was grateful Susanna had put her right.

Thanks to the many cold compresses

the lump had gone down on Lizzie's head and Thomas was much better, too.

It was only when the goats escaped and Lizzie was running round the yard laughing and trying to round them up with Thomas, Connor and Susanna that they realised they were all back to their normal cheerful selves.

On the evening before the wedding, the house was quiet. Lizzie had been dozing in front of the fire. Thomas was patrolling outside and Susanna was busy sewing away, while keeping one eye on Lizzie.

'Come on, girl, I need your help,' she said. Lizzie yawned and gave a big stretch.

'What for?' she asked.

Susanna held up a pretty cream gown.

'I've made it a little bit shorter so when you're wearing it to feed the goats or collect the eggs or muck out the stables, you won't get it so filthy.' Susanna smiled, pleased with her work.

'But you're to promise me not to do

any of those chores until after the wedding, I want you to walk down that aisle looking your best.'

Lizzie laughed and gave Susanna a hug.

'I'm sorry it didn't work out with Jeremiah,' Lizzie said quietly. 'I was fond of him, but I love Connor.'

'It pains me to say it but it's all turned out for the best. Connor is the right man for you and I still consider myself your mother-in-law. I shall look forward to being a grandmother to your children.'

Bad News

Lizzie carefully folded the dress and handed it back to Susanna so it would be ready for her wedding in the morning. They retired early to bed so as to be fresh for the wedding in the morning.

They were awakened later that night by the sound of hooves and Thomas's raised voice outside.

A messenger had been sent from the Hamilton ranch with news for them.

'Mr Hamilton senior sent me over, miss,' the rider said. 'He was sorry to send bad news on this night of all nights but thought you needed to know.'

The man paused. Thomas, Susanna and Lizzie all looked at each other and then back at the messenger. Lizzie's heart skipped a beat. Connor was staying at the ranch with May and

Duke and they were all travelling to the chapel together in the morning.

What if something awful had happened to Connor? Lizzie felt faint and reached out to steady herself.

'Come on, man, tell us the news,' Thomas urged. 'Tell us the worst.'

'We heard from young Mr Hamilton's men that he's been killed by a stampeding buffalo. He won't be returning home . . . ever.'

'Elijah? Killed?' Thomas gasped.

Lizzie hadn't realised it but she'd been holding her breath. She let out a deep sigh that Connor was unharmed. Then, almost immediately her thoughts turned to May.

'I must go to May,' she said. 'She'll want someone to comfort her.'

'Oh, no, you can't,' Susanna told her. 'For one thing, Connor is there and for another you must stay here for your own safety. What if it's all some almighty trap to kidnap you again?'

'But if Elijah is dead . . . ' Lizzie began.

'We don't know for sure it was him and we don't know if he'd made other plans to spoil this ceremony, too.'

'But surely everyone will know Elijah's gone and I don't think those men would carry out his wishes if they didn't have to. They were just doing as they were told.'

'You are too forgiving,' Susanna told her as she stood and went to fetch her cape. 'Thomas, can you spare your cart?'

'What for?'

'I want this young man,' she pointed to the messenger, 'to take me over to May. I'll sit with her tonight, but don't worry, I'll send word to Mary Franklin and she and I will come over early tomorrow and dress you for your wedding.'

Lizzie began to protest but Susanna held up her hand and Lizzie realised that for once she had to do as she was told.

* * *

The day dawned for wedding number two. The sun shone, the sky was a dazzling blue and the church bells began to ring.

Susanna Newham and Mary Franklin gave Lizzie one last hug and then hurried over the road to the chapel. Susanna hesitated at the door.

'I know,' Thomas said with a grin. 'I'm not to let her out to pet the goats, feed the chickens or collect eggs. Now be off with you. Let's get her wed and enjoy the dancing. I could certainly do with a drink.'

'No drink until the ceremony is over, Thomas, or I'll not be consenting to be your wife.'

'I haven't asked you,' Thomas said in surprise.

'No, that's true.' Susanna laughed. 'But you will.'

Lizzie was escorted from her homestead over the road to the little white chapel that stood on the hill at High Point. This time the road was quiet and someone had been out to dampen down the dust. It was a clear day and the posse of armed men around her could see for miles. The only thing that moved was a rabbit in the distance.

Just as they left the perimeter of the homestead a piercing scream filled the air.

'What on earth was that?' Thomas asked. His face pale, he held his gun up and looked around.

Lizzie laughed.

'That'll be Martha.'

'Martha?'

'One of the goats. I didn't think she was due to give birth just yet. I hope she's all right.' Lizzie turned back as if to go and check on her.

'Don't worry,' one of Duke's men said. 'I'll tend to her. I was brought up with goats. I'll make sure she's fine and when it's all over I'll send word so you know whether it's a billy or a nanny.'

Everyone laughed. Lizzie thanked the ranch hand and allowed herself to be escorted over the road to meet Connor, the man she loved and hoped to spend the rest of her life with.

This time the wedding went smoothly. Connor smiled at his beautiful bride and reached out for her hand as soon as she arrived beside him in church.

He had a relieved look on his face and Lizzie wondered if he too had heard Martha the goat call out and whether he too was wondering how she was faring.

There was much celebrating for the rest of the day. Mr King, as his wedding gift, had provided yet another enormous feast for everyone. There was plenty to drink and the band provided music for dancing.

'Mrs Riordan?' A stranger approached Lizzie with his hat in his hand. He looked as though he were going to ask her for a dance. Connor stood protectively by her side. Lizzie had never been called Mrs Riordan before and it took some moments for her to realise the man was addressing her.

'Yes?'

'John has sent word,' the stranger said. 'Martha is fine. You now have two more goats to add to the herd, one male and one female. He suggests you call them Bridie and Groom.'

'What a wonderful surprise wedding present.' Lizzie laughed and everyone raised their glasses to Bridie and Groom, the new goats.

'Make sure you take this jug of ale over to John and thank him for his help,' Connor said. 'And take him a plate of food, too. But make sure the goats don't get it.'

Before the evening was over there was more celebration. Thomas had seen Susanna in her finery and realised what a catch she was. Lizzie had noticed they had been deep in discussion for some time and had missed several dances.

'I wanted to be honest,' Thomas was telling the newly married couple. 'I told her I didn't know if I'd ever be able to settle down completely.'

'And what did she say?'

'She said if I ever needed to become

a pedlar again and to travel round she would be waiting for me when I returned but in the meantime I will give it a try to help out at Goat Corner and take our produce to market regularly.

'That might help me settle, but now and again it would be good to travel to other markets — especially with the things Susanna can sew.'

'And so when's your big day?' Lizzie asked Susanna.

'We're going to go and see the preacher now, tonight, before Thomas changes his mind.' Susanna laughed as she slipped her hand around her new love, and pulled him close.

Lizzie and Connor watched as they walked arm in arm back toward the chapel and to the dwelling next door where the preacher lived. He had been at the celebrations earlier but had retired early to bed, little knowing he would be disturbed.

The dancing was just starting up again when a hush came over the proceedings. A pale, tear-stained May stood at the entrance to the barn with Duke Hamilton beside her.

Lizzie had noticed they were both present at the chapel and for that she was surprised, but very grateful. Understandably they had not come along to the dancing, that was, until now.

'May,' Lizzie ran over to her and opened her arms to hug her friend.

'Can you ever forgive me?' May asked. 'I can't believe what Elijah has done. Reece has confessed to the whole thing. It was as we suspected.

'I don't know if he was responsible for the original fire. That secret will go to the grave with him but he was guilty of having you kidnapped and he'd told his men that if you died from being hit on the head, they were to leave you to the prairie dogs to finish you off.'

Lizzie shivered. Connor put an arm around her shoulders.

'I'm so sorry,' May said again. 'I had hoped we would always be firm friends.'

'And so we shall,' Lizzie reassured her. 'In fact we're now sisters and I shall expect we will visit each other daily.'

'I would love that.' May smiled and a little colour came to her cheeks.

'I told you she would say that,' Duke whispered. 'Didn't I say that Lizzie Holden — sorry, Riordan — was one very special woman?'

We do hope that you have enjoyed reading this large print book.

Did you know that all of our titles are available for purchase?

We publish a wide range of high quality large print books including:
Romances, Mysteries, Classics
General Fiction
Non Fiction and Westerns

Special interest titles available in large print are:
The Little Oxford Dictionary
Music Book, Song Book
Hymn Book, Service Book

Also available from us courtesy of Oxford University Press:
Young Readers' Dictionary
(large print edition)
Young Readers' Thesaurus
(large print edition)

For further information or a free brochure, please contact us at:
Ulverscroft Large Print Books Ltd.,
The Green, Bradgate Road, Anstey,
Leicester, LE7 7FU, England.
Tel: (00 44) **0116 236 4325**
Fax: (00 44) **0116 234 0205**

FIRESTORM

Alan C. Williams

1973: Debra Winters has started a new life for herself as a teacher in a small Australian outback town. Given the responsibility of updating the school's fire protocol, she is thrown together with volunteer firefighter Robbie Sanderson, and there's a spark of attraction between them. Meanwhile, things are heating up: it's bushfire season, and there's an arsonist on the loose. Debra and Robbie find themselves in danger. Will their relationship flicker out — or will they set each other's worlds alight?

A GIFT FOR CELESTINE

Sheila Daglish

The village of St Justin is happy for archaeologist Alex to create a festival exhibition in the chateau beside the Dordogne. The highlight of the display is a fabulous necklace, a gift for a local girl who, centuries ago, was loved by the lord's son. But the jewels bring danger for Alex — and to brooding vineyard owner Raoul. Raw from past betrayals, he denies his attraction to her even as they are drawn closer. But Alex knows there can be no true love, no future, for them without trust . . .

A WOMAN'S PLACE

Wendy Kremer

Sarah Courtney has lived with her aunt and uncle, a prosperous merchant, since her father died a year ago. When the handsome and wealthy Ross Balfour catches her eye, she has no expectation of marrying him — until they accidentally fall into a compromising situation, and he offers for her hand to save her reputation. Ross's plan is for the union to be a sham so that Sarah can receive her inheritance and fulfil her dream of opening an apothecary's shop. Love will never enter into it . . . or will it?